Dear Shezi,

A Kiss in Kashmir

Monica Saigal

Love,
Monica
2024

ISBN-13: 9780997662498
ISBN-13: 9798989708208 (ebook)

Cover designed by Humble Nations, Copyright © 2023
Formatting by Polgarus Studio

Bodes Well Publishing
Please contact publisher@bodeswellpublishing.com about special discounts for bulk purchases

Disclaimer

This is a work of fiction. Names, characters, businesses, places, events and incidents are either the products of the author's imagination or used in a fictitious manner. Any resemblance to actual persons, living or dead, or actual events is purely coincidental.

Advance Praise

"On the face of it, in *A Kiss in Kashmir*, Monica Saigal (Bhide) sets a sweet romance in a luscious setting. Looking deeper, it's a novel that explores the depth of loss, love, and the many facets of the human heart. Bravo." **—Mollie Cox Bryan, Agatha and Daphne du Maurier Award–nominated author**

"Monica Saigal (Bhide)'s latest novel brings to life the magic of Kashmir with its gorgeous colors, smells, and tastes. From the first page, you'll feel like you are at a banquet for the senses in this touching tale of later-life love and the hope of new beginnings."
—Ramin Ganeshram, author, *Saffron: A Global History*

"In *A Kiss in Kashmir*, Monica Saigal (Bhide) transports us to a place where the warmth of a pashmina meets the scent of saffron. Kashmir comes alive, not just as a backdrop but as a character, breathing life into Sharmila and George's journey. Their story reminds us that even after loss, love can find its way back. Saigal's tale is genuine, heartfelt, and flavored with the authentic touch of Kashmir. *A Kiss in Kashmir* is an intimate sojourn, promising the heart that love, in all its forms, can indeed find its way back to us." **—Chef and filmmaker Vikas Khanna**

Agar firdaus bar roo-e zameen ast,
Hameen ast-o hameen ast-o hameen ast.
(If there is a paradise on earth, it is this, it is this, it is this.)

–Amir Khusrau on Kashmir

This book is dedicated to you.

May all the love, abundance, and prosperity you desire be yours.

Prologue: 1995

Gawkadal Bridge, Srinagar, Kashmir

Vikram had never been happier. The air in Srinagar was just as he remembered it—crisp and hopeful. He looked up at the blue sky. It was the last time he would be here as a single man.

"Sometimes I wonder what I have done to deserve all this good fortune," he would tell anyone who was willing to listen—his painting students, the woman who delivered his tiffin (lunchbox) to his small room in Jaipur, the young kid who washed his landlord's cars, God (well, of course), and last but not the least, random tourists he met when he visited the many colorful palaces of Jaipur. At night, before closing his eyes, he often pinched himself to see if it was a dream or reality. Life had been kind and, he reminded himself on this cold October day, it was about to get remarkably more magical.

His parents in Srinagar had been upset on the phone earlier that week. "Vikram, stay in Jaipur. It isn't safe here. The insurgents are out in full force. Beta, son, listen to us," his mother pleaded with him over the phone.

"Ma, nothing will happen. You cannot possibly tell me to stay away from you and Baba. I have big news that I want to tell you in person." Vikram's voice, filled with sheer delight, eventually convinced his mother. "You will be so happy, Ma. It is all good news."

"*Beta, child, be careful. Come straight home from the station. Baba will not be able to get you this time. He isn't leaving the house now, you know, his legs ...*" Ma began to sob. Her husband's increasingly out-of-control diabetes had taken a toll on his legs.

"Fikar na karo, Ma, don't worry." Vikram beamed into the payphone. "The news I bring will have Baba dancing in no time. Ma, my paintings have been selling. I have made enough money now for us to get the best doctors to treat Baba. I have money now, you can rest easy. No more cooking for the world. And one more thing ... Ma? Ma? Can you hear me?"

The line went dead. Vikram was thrilled to be returning home. He hadn't been gone that long—just about eighteen months. The opportunity to teach art and painting in a small school in Jaipur had come up suddenly and by chance. His father's childhood friend, Rashid, owned the school and needed a substitute teacher in a pinch.

"I can teach oil, watercolor, and sketching. But my specialty is oil," Vikram had told Rashid uncle. Rashid uncle was well known and admired, and Vikram looked up to him.

Rashid had responded, "Your special talent, son, is your ability to see the beauty in this world. And that is what I am looking for in an instructor—to teach how to spot beauty. Techniques, anyone can teach them. You, however, train their soul to *see.*"

It was in Vikram's first week there that what had simply been an opportunity to teach turned into a sweet romance.

His mind floated back to the first time he saw her.

"I am told you are the best there is," Sharmila, a member of one of the most eminent royal families of Jaipur, had said to him when they were first introduced. She showed him some of her artwork. Her amateur work showed that she clearly had talent. But more than that, she had vision.

Soon, his tiny studio filled up with a handful of students. He tried to help them all, but his focus was always on Sharmila from the very first. She laughed easily, painted with abandon, and was curious about his life and his art. He often told her that there weren't enough hours in the day, or even a lifetime, to answer all her questions. Nevertheless, she would persist, her curiosity insatiable.

"Vikram, how does the sunrise differ in October versus January when you paint it? What does this brush do? How did you find that perfect shade of magenta?"

Of course, the questions slowly went from being about painting to him, and then to them.

"What is your dream, Vikram—for your art, I mean? Tell me about your mom. Does your brother paint? I eagerly wait for each morning to be with you, do you feel the same? Is this what love feels like? I feel so safe in your embrace, do you feel that?"

Endless questions, and each one drew him closer to her. He had many of his own.

"I worry I am not good enough for you, Sharmila. You belong to one of the richest families in the country and my family is from a small town. We are of humble means."

She would simply smile in response. And if he insisted on worrying, she would add, "I didn't fall in love with your bank balance, and I did not choose to be born into a royal family. Love is love. That is all that matters."

Their love of art, of the blank canvas and its promise, brought them closer and closer.

"You must learn to think and see with your brush. Your brush should lead your hand, not the other way around." Vikram guided her hand as she learned the intricacies of her craft. Within a short few weeks, her work had shown remarkable progress.

Vikram remembered how shocked he had been when she showed him a painting.

"Vikram, I want you to see something." Sharmila had pulled him into one of the many gardens behind the studio. She had spent early morning hours working on a mural. On a small wall, facing a fountain behind the studio, she had painted him standing by a lake with a brush in hand and canvas in front of him.

"Oh, this is beautiful. You make me look good," he had said, a bit shy at first.

"I did what you said. My brush guided me. This is the result."

He had kissed her that day and she had held him close, whispering, "I think I am falling in love with you."

Just the thought of her and her name made his smile brighter than the sun in Srinagar that morning.

But there was a stop he needed to make before heading home, right by the Gawkadal Bridge. The bridge had been the site of a massacre a few years earlier, a terrible memory. The last time Vikram had called home, his brother, Suraj, mentioned that the area was now safer, but added, "This isn't the Kashmir of our childhood. I know you will want to see Afzal for tosha, but come home first."

Vikram had mumbled an agreement, but of course disagreed

in his head. A typical artist, he always insisted that these political things were a passing phase and did not affect him. Besides, he had to tell his childhood friend, Afzal, about Sharmila. Of course, he also wanted to pick up tosha for his mother. Filled with cashews, almonds, and sugar, tosha was his mother's favorite treat. And pairing a sweet dish with good news was how he had been raised.

Vikram clutched his well-worn gray woolen scarf closer to his body and held his bag tight. The bag held a surprise for his parents, one he couldn't wait to share. It was true what his grandmother had always said: *Jahun chhuh ashhun mazhar* (the world is a theatre of love). Now, he could tell Ma and Baba about Sharmila, about *their* magical theatre of love that was his life. A life filled with colors, romance, promises of loving family, and a woman whose eyes were not something just to look at but to immerse your soul in. Everything about Sharmila was a gift from the Divine: the graceful way she twirled her paintbrush, the naughtiness with which she teased his desperate attempts at cooking her favorite dishes, the gentleness when her lips touched his, the softness of her hair as it fell on his face, the flowery smell of her perfume when he nuzzled her neck, the mole near her quivering lips that he kissed every opportunity he got. Soon now, she would be his. They had decided to wed in Kashmir in April, on Sharmila's birthday. He could hardly wait to tell his parents. The thought of seeing her in wedding finery with his family blessing them, and his beloved city surrounding them, made Vikram giddy with anticipation.

He smiled as he looked at the red and yellow autumn leaves falling around him. He had told Sharmila all about autumn there and had even taught her to paint these leaves. He enjoyed painting a verbal picture of his favorite places in Kashmir and then watched her paint those landscapes. She was a quick learner and could paint majestic scenes with ease.

"What color exactly was the tree bark? How did the sky look from this angle? How many minarets were there in the mosque? How many steps were there in that temple?" Sharmila and her never-ending questions created magic on the canvas.

He remembered their first trip outside of Jaipur. Sharmila had been telling him about the little sacred town of Pushkar, a blessed town nestled in the heart of her home state of Rajasthan.

"I want to take you there and show you Pushkar Lake, Vikram. While it isn't like the Dal Lake of your beautiful Kashmir, I know you will love it. There is something timeless about it. I love walking in Pushkar, with all the sound of the chanting, the smell of the incense and endless number of divine places. Oh, *and* the hot air balloons."

The balloon ride over Pushkar was nothing like he had ever experienced before. While Pushkar itself had been intoxicating, the balloon ride was extraordinary. The balloons danced to the rhythm of the air and every view was breathtaking.

He said as he held her close, "This balloon makes me feel like I am a part of the canvas of this landscape, this desert below, that lake, the labyrinthine, colorful streets, that warm sun."

After the ride, he had put his secret plan into action. He'd worked with Sharmila's sister to make sure nothing would go wrong.

He had taken her to a small open-air theatre that hosted traditional Rajasthani puppet shows. They found seats on the first wooden bench. All the benches were full as locals and tourists alike came to watch the sweet performances.

"Oh, I have loved these since I was a child!" Sharmila exclaimed.

At first, Sharmila didn't seem to notice. Then it suddenly dawned on her—the puppets on stage, large, intricate marionettes dressed in vibrant Rajasthani clothes, were telling her and Vikram's love story, from the time they met to the present moment. Just under a year, but a memorable and beautiful year. The dialogues were accompanied by musicians playing the double-headed drum dholak and the stringed instrument, the sarangi. Oil lamps strung around the stage and the entire theatre cast gentle light and dramatic shadows.

As the puppet show reached its climax, the male puppet hesitated, then offered something in his hand to the female puppet. He then told the audience, "For the rest of the show, please watch the couple on the first bench."

Vikram turned to Sharmila and said, "I don't have the riches of the world, but I love you dearly and promise to make you the happiest woman on earth. Will you marry me?" In his hand, much to her delight, instead of a ring he was holding his favorite and most prized paintbrush.

While the audience clapped and called for rings to be exchanged, teary-eyed Sharmila lovingly accepted the valued brush and hugged her husband-to-be.

***

The memory made him smile. And now, soon, he would bring her here to his hometown of Srinagar, in his beautiful state of Kashmir. It would be her first time. He couldn't wait. He knew she would fall in love with the valley as soon as she saw it.

Vikram's senses were in overdrive as thoughts of Sharmila filled every cell of his body. The bridge was just ahead. He could see a large crowd had gathered—there appeared to be a protest of some sort. It was fairly common, so he thought nothing of it. He simply shook his head. His homeland needed peace. All these political rallies, all these people shouting slogans. He often wondered why there was so much hatred. His precious valley needed peace. Perhaps, he prayed, it would come soon. All this violence had just created much more of the same.

The sounds of the protests grew, and Vikram tried to ignore them. He went deeper into his daydreams about Sharmila and how excited his parents would be to hear the good news of his impending nuptials. He knew they would have the same concerns about her royal background, but he felt in his heart that he would be able to convince them.

Suddenly the screams and slogan-chanting around him grew louder, and Vikram heard shots. He thought he heard a familiar voice—was it Afzal's?—screaming to *him* to stay away from the bridge. He turned to see several women running to cross the street. Then he saw the sign for Afzal's shop. It was now a burnt-out wreck where it had once stood so proudly. And his friend lay dead in front of it.

Vikram ran towards Afzal. He bent over the sprawled figure and began to weep as chaos reigned around him. A man yelled slurs at him, but in all the noise Vikram couldn't hear what he was saying. Then he looked up at men holding guns and his eyes widened with a flicker of recognition. A barrage of bullets hurtled toward him.

Vikram's bag flew out of his hands as he fell, his head hitting the ground. People were running—frenzied screaming, death cries. Then an abrupt quiet. Passersby rapidly skirted Vikram's quivering body. His eyes blinked and he cried out in pain. He reached out to the sky, begging for help. The contents of his bag had spilled onto the street. Peeking out was a painting of a young woman with lustrous hair, a radiant smile, a mole on the right side of her lip, and her hands on her belly, as though protecting the life that was growing inside her.

Chapter 1

October 2022
Srinagar, Kashmir

"Mr. Rami, this isn't what you promised us."

An exasperated Sharmila tried to maintain her grace as she struggled to inform the wedding planner that all his information so far had been, well, useless. He had been showing them photos of the ballrooms of large hotels, and some random farmhouses that were exorbitantly priced but had little or no cultural significance.

"Madam ji, koi baat nahi, no problem. I will show you more. But I am telling you, no one in Kashmir Valley will support a wedding in winter like you are saying you want. And even early spring will be hard. Outdoor photo shoots will be hard. Your guests, madam ji, they may not even be able to get here … the snowfall still sometimes comes in March. All the outdoor venues you want are good, but the hotels are better." Rami Sarkar tried hard to be polite. This was his business, and he knew what he was doing. These westernized Indians were worse than actual westerners. *These NRI's think they know everything,* Mr. Rami thought behind his smile. He knew the city of Srinagar better than all of them and he was annoyed that they didn't respect his recommendations. "Madam ji, I am telling you, the hotel catering will also be great. It will be easy for you. No extra planning."

Sharmila tried to be polite but firm too. "Mr. Rami, this is not acceptable. I want to see the various sights that I mentioned to you over the phone."

They were standing at the edge of Dal Lake in Srinagar as a gentle breeze, carrying scents of tea brewing on the stalls nearby, tickled their noses.

Mr. Rami pushed a little harder. "Madam ji, I will see what I can find. The hotels are lovely here. You must—" Before he could complete his sentence, Alina piped up.

"Ma, look, look at the lake, Ma—there are white swans. A whole family of them."

Sharmila turned to look where her daughter was pointing. A gentle calm instantly came over her.

The October morning sun spread its cozy rays over Dal Lake as the mountains beyond embraced the water as if to bless and call it their own. Colorful shikaras, flat-bottomed wooden boats with elegant, curvy designs, filled the lake as tourists poured in, trying to capture some of the magic in their hearts, but mostly on their phone cameras.

Right in the middle of it all, a family of snow-white swans was swimming towards one of the patches of floating garden that naturally grew in the lake. The scene was one that Vikram's words had imprinted in her memory, his words from over two decades ago, *There is nothing in this world like Dal Lake. If you look carefully, you would think that God has played favorites here.*

Sharmila was glad that Alina had found something to make her smile. She had been hard to deal with the past few weeks, ever since Sharmila suggested she have her wedding in India, and particularly in the last two days since they'd arrived. Alina was not thrilled at the idea of getting married in a country neither she nor her fiancé, Emilio, had ever been to before. Sharmila insisted that Alina at least give it a chance. Alina had agreed on the condition that she would have the final say and that she wanted a wedding in the US as well.

Sharmila took a deep breath. "Mr. Rami, I have paid you to show me the area, some of the monuments, and maybe a heritage hotel that can be good for the wedding, and we really need to do some wedding shopping. I wish you would do just that. I have mentioned that we are flexible with the dates—maybe winter, or an early spring wedding. It will be so unusual, amidst the snow-capped mountains, the chilly breeze, and the magical ambiance."

"Madam ji, shall I make an appointment with the Chinar Hotel? They will take care of everything. You won't need to plan anything yourself—henna, sangeet, the wedding."

"I don't know how to explain to you that I don't *want* the Chinar Hotel," Sharmila said yet again.

Alina was back to being irritated. "Ma, I told you we shouldn't have come. I mean, how can I give anything a chance here when I haven't seen a single interesting thing? Mr. Rami, I don't want a hotel in the middle of nowhere. I don't know anything about this place." She turned back to her mother. "Ma, I know you want a Kashmiri wedding, but can't we do it back home in Washington? We could easily find a Kashmiri planner there."

The spell of the peaceful lake was broken, and Sharmila became visibly frustrated.

"Mr. Rami, how many times did I tell you on the phone that we wanted to tour the valley and see it before we decide what to do and where? I don't want some random hotel catering, I don't want a choreographed sangeet in some nondescript ballroom. Why can't we see options? Why are you insistent on this one single hotel?" Sharmila's voice rose slightly as she tried to restrain herself.

"But madam ji, I am not a tour guide. I am a wedding planner and I have a plan here, ready for you. I have already done the work. All you have to do is come see the venue and then sign the wedding contract with the hotel."

"That is *not* what you said on the phone. You promised me that we could visit the specific sites that I had suggested, and then we could decide what to do. Also, Mr. Rami, I do not see any outdoor options on that list you sent me." Sharmila reached into her purse and waved a piece of paper in Mr. Rami's face.

"Madam ji, you will have shivering guests, your bride will be cold in her lovely bridal attire. I cannot recommend anything outdoors. Also, while the historical locales are undoubtedly impressive, hosting a wedding there can be quite challenging due to logistics. I have just the gem for you. But we must—"

Despite being just as disappointed, Alina tried to lighten the mood as she saw her mom getting more agitated. "Oh, come on. If we need to, we'll provide adorable blankets, fluffy earmuffs for the guests—it'll be an experience they'll never forget. Besides, whichever kind of wedding dress I wear, I can always wear thermal leggings underneath. We just want to see options and then we can decide."

Mr. Rami was adamant, further annoyed, and at this point exasperated by the mother-daughter duo. "Alina ji, this is not funny. I am a serious wedding planner. I will be blamed if the wedding is bad. In all my good conscience, I cannot recommend any outdoor site for even a short while when it is cold out. What will you do for flowers? We may not be able to get what you want. And that is *if* your guests can come to Kashmir. I am a simple, old-fashioned man and I'm trying to save you some headaches, but you don't want to even try to understand my point of view."

Alina kept her tone soft, trying to help Sharmila make her case. "See, Mr. Rami—this is our first visit to Kashmir. Now, if *you* visited a place for the first time, wouldn't you want to see the sights and learn about the culture before just rushing into a cookie-cutter hotel?"

"I am sorry … you want a hotel that has a cookie? Is that like a biscuit? I am sorry, I don't understand your requests." Mr. Rami was sweating now even in this cool morning, and used his sleeve to wipe the sweat off his forehead. "I am not sure what you want, madam ji. We are not having cookie hotels here. What is that?"

His pathetic expression and sad voice suddenly made both Alina and Sharmila laugh.

Poor man, Sharmila thought, *perhaps I'm expecting too much from him. I wonder what I can do now?*

"Excuse me, ma'am?" Mother and daughter both turned around to see two men standing behind them, drinking kahwa, the traditional Kashmiri tea, from a pushcart vendor.

"Please, let us welcome you to our valley," one of the men

said. "Before I say anything more, may I offer you some delicious Kashmiri tea from my friend's tea cart here? A cup of this magical tea settles a lot." The man's smile and gentle demeanor made Sharmila smile, but she hesitated.

Alina said quickly, "Oh, yes please. Ma has been telling me about this tea forever. I guess it was my father's favorite—this is the one with the rose petals and saffron, right? I researched it and tried to make it. It was, well, a disaster. It tasted more like spicy hot water than tea." Alina brushed aside her long curls and reached out to shake hands.

"Alina, we don't know these people," Sharmila whispered, but then almost instinctively let it go. Alina was outgoing, always had been, and at twenty-six she was a bit too old for lectures about being wary of strangers.

The stranger accepted her hand. "It is nice to meet you. I am Wajid Malik, and this is my brother, George Tomson. Welcome to my home, welcome to the valley."

Wajid slowly shifted, and as he did, George emerged into Sharmila's view. Her reaction was immediate. A warm, charming smile spread across her face as she was momentarily taken aback by his good looks. He was dressed in a charcoal-gray wool sweater and well-fitting jeans that had a worn-in look. On his feet, he sported a pair of rugged, brown leather boots. His salt-and-pepper hair peeking out from under a baseball cap and a close-trimmed beard added a distinguished touch. With his blue eyes and pale Caucasian skin, he appeared to be just another Western tourist, albeit a remarkably attractive one, a fact Sharmila couldn't deny as her gaze lingered on him.

Fortunately, Alina was still being forward. "It's nice to meet you too, Wajid. I'm Alina Solanki, and this is my mom, Sharmila Solanki. You have a white brother?" Alina had zero filters. Sharmila tugged at her daughter's shirt to gently chide her.

George smiled and extended his hand. "Hah. Well, he is actually my brother-in-law, but more like a brother." Sharmila smiled back at him as she took it. *He has such a powerful grip*, she thought.

"And here is some tea." Wajid handed tea to the ladies and a very exasperated Mr. Rami, who reluctantly accepted it.

The group stood quietly for a few moments and sipped as they watched the swans swim up close. The chatter of the vendors selling everything from silver jewelry to water lilies to palm reading was growing louder and louder as tourists began to make their way towards the lake. Large families with older parents, children of varying ages, school groups, and more began to swarm the area. It had been years since the valley had seen this many visitors. The new government was doing its best to bring back tourism after years of problems, and it was, by all accounts, succeeding.

Frowning, Mr. Rami took the opportunity to check his phone.

It was George who broke the silence. "We overheard your conversation. It appears you are looking for an experienced tour guide? Wajid here offers historical tours of the valley, if that is what you are looking for."

Alina beamed at George. "Are you from DC? I see you're wearing a Nationals cap."

"Oh, I love the Nationals and yes, I grew up in DC. But I was born in Hyannis in Massachusetts. You know, like the Kennedys."

Alina smiled. "Nice. We're visiting from DC, and I went to

Boston College. What a coincidence."

"I guess it *is* a small world. I did grad work in Boston. Well, Cambridge, actually, but Boston College is a great school," George said. "Now, what's going on with this gentleman here?"

"Oh, you see, my mother has a deep sentimental attachment to the idea of having my wedding ceremony in India, particularly here in Kashmir," Alina explained. "Mr. Rami's been kind enough to offer his assistance, but it's becoming apparent that my mother's cherished vision and Mr. Rami's proposals are a world apart."

Exasperated, Mr. Rami said, "That is not fair, Alina ji, I am trying to help. If you could just see the Chinar Hotel. This is the hidden gem I am trying to tell you about. It is truly stunning, and the ballroom has hosted so many Bollywood weddings. Here, see the pictures." Mr. Rami thrust his iPhone under Alina's nose. She gently pushed it away.

"Okay, okay," Wajid said. "I don't mean to insert myself here, but as George said, I do give tours of this area. I have done so for over twenty years and would be happy to help you." This was much to the annoyance of Mr. Rami, who began to rant loudly. "You cannot do this. This is my customer. What is your name? Wajid? Wajid what? You cannot simply take my customers away."

Alina ignored him. "Oh, Ma, we should do the tour with them. We can see everything. I don't know about a wedding here, but maybe at least we can get a good tour."

Before Sharmila could respond, Mr. Rami erupted again. "You *cannot* take my customer. I will take you to the police. How can you do this? This is my customer. From America. *My* customer. Not yours. Find your own customers."

Passersby stopped to see what was going on and to eavesdrop on the unfolding drama. Wajid politely asked them to keep moving.

"It is just a tour, Mr. Rami," he said. "Why are you getting so upset? I am not a wedding planner like you."

But Mr. Rami was not having any of this. "Do you know who my brother is? He is a high police officer, the senior-most officer here at the main prison. I will get you arrested. I will call my brother. He has power. He will shut down your tourism business."

Sharmila heard Alina disguise a laugh with a cough.

Finally, George stepped in. "Sir, what is your consulting fee? She has paid you already, yes?" With a knowing glance at Sharmila, he went on, "Can I suggest that perhaps you can keep that as a cancellation fee and then you can go ahead and sell your services to people who better appreciate what you do? Clearly these ladies cannot see the amazing value you bring. I've seen the Chinar Hotel and I agree with you. It *is* gorgeous." Now George winked at Alina.

Alina looked at her mother. "Yes, yes, we will let you keep your fee. Ma, can't we do that?"

Sharmila was grateful for George's intervention and couldn't wait to get rid of this man who had offered no value in the past two days in the city. More importantly, this was the first time Alina seemed willing to explore the area. Alina had been reluctant to even come to India, let alone get married here, and had been moping as Mr. Rami had simply been meeting them for lunch and trying to convince them to see the one hotel and meet with just one caterer.

"Yes, I *will* keep my fees. You will all regret this. These tour guides don't know anything. But madam ji, it is your choice." Mr. Rami seemed relieved that he would be able to leave these demanding foreigners who knew nothing. *Who hosts an outdoor wedding in Kashmir in winter or so soon after winter? This was crazy. They don't know anything.* He left, still grumbling to himself.

Sharmila turned her attention to Wajid and George. "Thank you for your help. As I am assuming you overheard, we're here planning Alina's wedding. We want to explore the valley and find just the right spot to host the ceremony. We want it to have all the cultural elements of this amazing place—the food, the jewelry, the traditions. That's very important to me." Sharmila gave them her incandescent smile, a smile that lit up her eyes.

George couldn't help but smile back at this diminutive woman in her long, flowing pink dress draped with a light sky-blue cashmere shawl.

"That sounds excellent," Wajid said. "But if it's okay, may I ask, why Kashmir? I mean, I love my birthplace and home. I'm just curious as to why you chose this place?"

Alina said, "Oh, my father was from here. We want to honor his memory, and having it here makes Ma feel like he'll be part of the celebration." Then she asked for more tea.

"And who is the lucky man you'll be marrying?" George asked.

"His name is Emilio. He's in law school so he couldn't come with us. Want to see some photographs?" Alina had already pulled out her phone and was soon sharing pictures with Wajid and George.

Sharmila took another sip of her tea and sighed in relief.

Perhaps this was for the best. Or was it? She'd stopped taking risks a long time ago, and this *was* risky. Agreeing to take a tour with a man they'd just met on the side of the lake, in a state she didn't know? This was likely insane. Her apprehension must have shown on her face.

George told her gently, "Sharmila, you can search for Wajid and his company online and check out the reviews. You will be in good, safe, and knowledgeable hands."

Within a few seconds, Alina was on her phone reading the Yelp reviews for Wajid Malik's tours. "Knowledgeable, helpful, honest … and 'treats you like family.' Oh, and I love this part: 'He knows all of the beloved food spots in Srinagar.' I can't wait to try the food here. This is terrific. These are great reviews, Ma."

Sharmila and Alina began making plans with Wajid for him to meet them at their hotel the next morning at nine to start a tour that would take them to all the places that Sharmila had heard about from Vikram. Finally, after so many years, she and Alina would be seeing it all in person.

"Well, Ma, looks like Dad is watching over us. He must've known that that Rami dude didn't really know anything, and now we have Wajid." Alina appeared delighted as she called her fiancé. "Emilio? When are you leaving Rome? How is your nonna now?"

Despite law school, Emilio had flown to Italy for a few days to be with his grandmother, who needed emergency heart surgery. All had gone well, and she was now recovering.

Alina stayed on the phone as Sharmila confirmed everything with Wajid and they exchanged contact information.

As the two ladies began to walk back to their hotel, Sharmila couldn't help herself, and discreetly turned to look back at George, even as she couldn't quite believe she was doing it. Was she really, actually, reacting to a man? At her age?

As she looked at him, she saw that he was looking at her. Quickly she turned back and increased her pace. Still, she admitted to herself that even at that first glance, she'd felt something tugging at her heart.

But surely this was stupid? Here she was, at her time in life, looking at a man—and a possibly married man at that. What was she thinking? This was crazy. Perhaps it was the intoxicating valley that was making her look at this handsome fellow. Yes, that was it. It was the valley. Vikram always said that. *The valley was intoxicating.*

For a moment, Sharmila wondered if there was such a thing as love at first sight. Was it possible for the cosmos to create chaos in hearts in a single meeting? Was it possible for eyes to meet and hearts to melt in a single glance? Were mystic unions only in poetry and fiction—or in real life too? Could a soul connect with another based on a single look?

Even as the questions swirled in her head, she cast them aside. This was silliness.

This will pass, she told herself.

That night, as Sharmila fell asleep, the last thoughts she had were of shaking hands with George, of his firm grip, his blue eyes looking into hers, his salt-and-pepper beard and hair.

And she wondered, quietly and with some guilt, what it would be like to kiss him.

Chapter 2

The Next Day

"Ma, you look radiant this morning," Alina said admiringly. Sharmila had draped herself in her favorite blue pashmina over a white sweater and jeans, keeping in mind the dropping temperatures outside.

"You, my child, are such a delight. You're the one who looks radiant for your wedding planning. I'm just along for the ride," Sharmila said.

"And the bills, Ma, you're here to pay the *bills*." Both of them laughed as they quickly finished their breakfast—the hotel's Western-style buffet was a poor substitute for the traditional Kashmiri fare they wanted to taste, but they were excited at what Wajid would be showing them, and little bothered them this morning.

"I'm happy to see that you're at least a bit excited about this now, Alina. I am sorry, I don't mean to push this on you. I just feel so deeply that if your father were alive, he would've wanted this," Sharmila said as she finished the last sip of her unsweetened coffee. Sharmila worried that she was being like her parents, wanting her daughter to have a traditional wedding. She was about to voice her concern, when Alina spoke up again.

"Ma, I *am* happy to visit here and learn about Dad's culture. I'm just a bit unsure about having the wedding here. I do agree that Dad would've wanted this, given his love of the valley. I promise to keep an open mind," Alina said warmly. "Also, look at this. Wajid has awesome reviews on so many travel websites. Someone even said that he sings songs during the shikara rides. Just like the guys who sing in the gondolas in Venice. Emilio will love that. It reminds me of when he proposed to me on a gondola in Venice. *That* was amazing." Alina had been up late reading through the reviews and, of course, texting Emilio the minute-by-minute update on their Kashmiri adventure, which so far had been anything but.

As Sharmila finished her coffee, she wondered, just for a fleeting second, if George would come with Wajid.

"I wonder if George will come with Wajid?" Alina said, as if reading her mom's mind. "He seemed really nice."

"Why? He isn't the guide. I hope Wajid is as good as all those reviews you've been reading, Alina. Maybe I should have planned better? I just don't know if this is a good idea." Sharmila waved her manicured hand to the waiter that they were done. Alina shook her head and rolled her eyes.

They stepped outside the hotel and waited under the hotel's large awning. The canvas sheltered visitors from the hot sun, the cold rains, but more importantly, from bird poop. Before it was installed, a flock of the vibrantly colored Kalij pheasants had decided that the roof over the hotel entrance was the perfect place to build their nests. Several attempts to remove the nests had failed. In addition, the birds were so beautiful, almost like peacocks in their appearance, that many hotel guests wanted to see them. But the birds, well, pooped. The hotel was inundated with complaints about bird poop falling on the shoulders and hair of guests. The final straw was when a baby bird fell down and stopped a very superstitious sports superstar in his tracks. He cancelled his reservation, because he took that as a sign of bad luck. Within hours, the awning had gone up.

Alina was the first to spot the Jeep. Driving it was George.

"Good morning, ladies," George said as he pulled up in front of them and popped out. "There's been a slight change. I am so, so sorry. I am afraid Wajid can't make it."

"What happened? Where is Wajid?" Sharmila was clearly irked, but seeing George's bright smile held her back from declaring this a complete and total disaster.

"Wajid had a nasty fall last night. At first we thought it was just a bad sprain, but it isn't. He went to the hospital early this morning and turns out it's a small hairline fracture of his left ankle. A tour guide who can't walk along with you isn't much use, I'm afraid." George stuffed his hands in his pocket. "I'm here to give you options. We can get you a tour guide from another company or, well, there is another option, but ... even I'm not sure about that."

Sharmila muttered, "Another company? Oh, my. This is getting to be such a mess again. Why can't one simple thing work out?"

Alina was annoyed too but wanted to hear what George was proposing. "What's the second option? I'm sorry Wajid fell. Kinda inconvenient, but whatever."

Sharmila said quickly, "Of course, I'm sorry to hear about Wajid as well. Now, getting another guide—I mean, how reliable will they be? I don't want to waste yet another day. We have such a short time left, and I just don't know ..." Sharmila found herself locked into his deep blue eyes. She hurriedly looked away.

"Then let me just offer option two. I'm happy to be your guide. I'm not a tour guide or a wedding planner by any stretch of the imagination, but I do know and love this valley. I've lived here on and off for many years. I got married in Srinagar. For what it's worth, I've accompanied Wajid on tours many times. I know I can help in finding you options that you'll like for venues, food—and heck, I even know where to buy wedding clothes," George said warmly.

Sharmila looked unsure, yet her heart was beating fast. She hoped Alina didn't notice that her hesitancy was turning into anticipation.

"You?" Sharmila asked, not wanting to appear overeager.

"Sharmila, I've known this valley for decades. I know many of the local vendors. If it helps you make a decision, I do have a doctorate in Indian art history. I must say, though, that I can't sing as well on the shikaras like Wajid does. The singing, he often says, is key to understanding the soul of a place. That's his claim to fame on social media, as I'm sure you've seen. In all fairness, since I can't sing well, I won't charge you a fee."

Alina laughed and her eyes lit up. "Ma, come on. This will be fun—a tour by Dr. George? How can that be boring?"

George said, "Yeah, I know more about Dal Lake than I do about Cape Cod at this point. I can get you the best kahwa in town, and yes, I do love kahwa more than Dunks." George and

Alina connected as George poked fun at Dunkin' coffee, from a homegrown Boston chain and very popular all over the world.

Sharmila was pleased that Alina seemed quite at home with George. Perhaps just trusting the universe at this point was the way to go. Alina leaned close and whispered in her mother's ear.

"He's so nice and so sweet. How bad can it be, Ma? Say yes."

Sharmila laughed. "All right, fine. Where do we start? Can we still go now? And, by the way, please give Wajid our best wishes. I will hold onto the no-fee offer and see how you do."

"Oh, before we start, Wajid sent this for you. It is our famous noonchai, a salted pink Kashmiri tea. It is made with green tea and Himalayan salt. Alina, he said you mentioned you loved food, so he wanted to start you all off with this lovely tea." George reached into the Jeep and pulled out a thermos. He passed out small terracotta cups and filled them.

"This is wonderful. I've never tasted anything like it," Sharmila said, and Alina nodded her agreement. "All right, you have won me over with the tea. Can we start now, George?"

"Yes, ma'am, we can start now. There's no better place to start than Dal Lake, of course. We have to start where it all begins. I have my shikara man waiting. When do you plan to fly in for the wedding? Though I must say, you have picked a cold time to get married. I mean, do you know what it's like here at the beginning of spring?"

"Yes, I know, it's after chillai kalan … I mean, if I remember correctly," Sharmila said, walking towards the Jeep. "It's still a time when the pheran and—"

"And the kangri are out. I'm impressed," George nodded. "Do you know what that means, Alina? No? Chillai kalan literally translates to *forty days of intense cold.* It starts on December 20th but can last well into March. But don't worry. If it is an early spring wedding you want, it is an early spring wedding you will have."

"What's a pheran? And that other thing you said? I want to look them up." Alina pulled out her phone.

"Pheran is a tunic-like outfit that's worn during the winters, and the kangri is a clay pot covered in wicker, that holds—wait for it—hot coals. It's worn under the pheran," George said.

"Wait, what? People literally wear hotpots under their clothes? How is that, like, legal? Isn't that a fire hazard? Wouldn't you burn yourself? Do *you* wear it?" Alina's questions continued. George laughed as he got them settled in the Jeep.

"Nah, I love this place but that's something I've never done. Wajid swears by his, though. Don't worry, we won't force you to wear that under your wedding dress. Although I have to say that the hotpot, as you called it, would've come in handy during the winter games in Foxboro."

"Wait, you're a Pats fan, too? I *love* the Pats. I even took Ma to a game once when she came up from DC to visit me at school. Though I think she ended up liking the quarterback more than the actual game," Alina said, giggling.

George caught sight of Sharmila blushing. "I think many women had a little bit of a crush on him, although they may not have admitted it. All right, here we go. I'll take you via the scenic route. I want to show you some of the sights of Srinagar before we get to Dal Lake."

The charming valley seemed to be in a mood to welcome visitors as the blue sky glittered. The gentle breeze wafted with scents of kebabs being cooked on the side of the road.

George gracefully navigated the Jeep, taking the time to highlight several landmarks along the route. Before long, they arrived at Nishat Bagh, an exquisite garden gracing the eastern shore of Dal Lake.

"This garden is not only remarkable for the way it was built, but it is a must-see for an outdoor wedding. I hope this will be a good start," he said as he helped Sharmila and Alina down and began to lead them to the garden. "I chose this one to be the first stop since the name means Garden of Joy. A lovely place to begin a life together, yes?"

The garden, George explained, was renowned for its twelve cascading terraces, colorful flowerbeds, and splendid views of Dal Lake and the Zabarwan mountain range. It was built, he added, by the Mughals in the early sixteen-hundreds.

Sharmila added, "The Mughal affinity for symmetry and precision shows up in the garden designs, Alina. See that? The central water channel flows through the terraces. The way it is built, it takes advantage of the best nature has to offer."

Alina stopped and stared at her mom. "Wow, Ma. I had no clue you knew so much about Kashmir. It's hard to believe you've never been here. I mean, I guess Dad must've told you stuff and all but—" Alina stopped as she saw the sadness on Sharmila's face.

George grinned. "Wait, wait, Sharmila. Don't add so much great information to my tour. For one, you make me look like I don't know what I'm talking about, and secondly, this makes me want to make you the tour guide and pay *you* the fees. Wajid will not be pleased if I do that." George winked again at Alina.

They walked the lush gardens. The tour buses had not arrived yet and so they had what seemed like a private tour of the garden.

Sharmila said, "These places are etched in my mind from so long ago. I'm not even sure if half of what I remember is correct. But I am glad to know that I haven't lost my memory … yet. Even though Alina thinks I'm ancient at fifty."

George told her, "Well then, we can be ancient together. My birthday is in three days, and I'll be turning fifty-*three*."

George's lighthearted manner appealed to Sharmila. It had been ages, maybe decades, since she'd even allowed herself to look at a man. There had been one tumultuous, short relationship after she moved to DC. She'd found herself trying hard with the new man in hopes of filling the large void Vikram had left in her heart. There was just no chemistry. It ended almost as soon as it had begun. *I can't be the Band-Aid for your heart, Sharmila. You need therapy*, were the man's last words to her. Her friends tried to set her up on dates; she had even gone on a few, as she worried that Alina needed a father figure. But that ended when one man announced that he wasn't on the market for her "daddy shopping" adventures. After that, a part of Sharmila decided that perhaps love was not in the cards. And yet, here she was, fifty years old and feeling giddy when she looked at this kind and gentle man.

Sharmila was so lost in her thoughts that she didn't even hear George calling her name.

"Sharmila? Sharmila? Hey."

Alina told him, "Oh, don't worry, George. Ma does that sometimes. She goes off into her imagination and I'm left here on Earth, wondering which planet she's visiting. By the look on her face this time, at least she isn't visiting her favorite planet: the land of stress and anxiety."

"Hah, very funny, Alina. What were you saying, George?"

"For what it's worth, I'm very familiar with that planet. Why don't you take a few photos and then we can continue on to Dal Lake?" George said. "Also, Alina, if you want an outdoor wedding here, may I make another suggestion? We won't be able to see it now, but I think it would be worth you looking it up on your phone."

Alina pulled out her phone and nodded.

"Check the Indira Gandhi Memorial Tulip Garden," he said. "It is better than any tulip garden in the world and in April, it is in full bloom. The gardens in Amsterdam are no match for the tulips here."

"*Omigod.* Ma, look at these pictures. What a riot of colors. It says here that there are over sixty varieties. I had no idea tulips came in that many. Thanks, George, already this is so exciting."

George was delighted. He continued to tell them more about the garden and the tulips and offered to take a few pictures with Sharmila's phone.

When he handed the phone back, Alina quickly browsed through the photos. "Wow, Ma. George takes amazing pictures. Look at how beautiful you look in these."

A half-hour later, they were back in the Jeep and on their way.

"Ladies, do you see that small building there? That used to be a palace. It was called the Pamposh Mahal. Do you know what pamposh means, Alina?" George pointed to a building covered in scaffolding, debris all around. It looked like the roof had caved in. A group of workers were calling out instructions to each other.

"I can find out in a minute on my phone, but I'm guessing

you want to tell me." Alina waved her phone at George.

"Thank you for letting me show off what I know. Pamposh is the name of the Kashmiri lily." George pulled the Jeep to the side of the road, directly in front of Pamposh Mahal.

"I've never heard of that." Sharmila looked at the building, which appeared newish in construction. "Well, I mean this is my first time here and I am sure there are so many places I don't know about."

George turned serious. "Yes, it's called Pamposh Mahal and it was said that the king who lived in it abdicated the throne when his queen died. It's rumored that he died of a broken heart. But then, it's also rumored that he died of overindulgence with the fairer sex when he tried to find someone to replace his queen. Anyway, the short of it is that the throne was then taken over by his daughter who, it was said, had fallen in love with a man who was the illegitimate son of the king. A son that the king had fathered with one of the ladies-in-waiting." George pointed to the various parts of the palace and explained a few more things about the illicit relationships of the princess and the craziness of those who lived in the palace.

"Wow, I had no idea that all this existed. I'm learning something new," Sharmila said as she removed her shawl. It was getting warm.

"Oh, yes, this place has history that you won't find in any books, or even on Google," George went on. "The actor Shah Rukh Khan—our beloved SRK—is all set to make a movie about this. You know, he once said in an interview that he would never come to Kashmir because he promised his father he would visit only with him? But his father died early and so SRK never came here. But it's said that once he heard this story, he changed his mind and decided to bring in his entire team—he'll be here next week to shoot. The palace also offers ghost tours. They say that the princess roams the halls at night, calling out for the lover who could never be hers. Yep, they never got married, because the citizens of the kingdom banned her from marrying the man when it was discovered he was her half-brother."

"Now, that *is* a crazy story. What was the name of the king? Which year did all this happen?" Sharmila took some pictures of the palace.

"That really is a wacky story, all right," Alina said. "This building doesn't look like a real palace though. Perhaps it's just old?"

"I have never heard about *any* of this," Sharmila said, frowning in concentration.

George could no longer hold back and began to laugh. "Well, you don't know about it because it never really happened. I'm just trying to give you something your wedding planner couldn't give you—some entertainment."

Sharmila was stumped for a second but then looked at Alina, who was laughing too.

Perhaps this misadventure was just what the two of them needed.

Chapter 3

Dal Lake

Dal Lake sparkled in the autumn sun. Several wooden boats, shikaras, glided across the lake with ease. Tourists were back in droves here too and the shikara boatmen were calling out to them to come take a ride in paradise. Each boat was unique, decorated with brightly colored canopies, comfortable seating with large pillows, and an elegantly curved hull. Many of the shikaras had vendors selling flowers and vegetables.

"Be careful as you step in, these shikaras have a mind of their own." George offered Sharmila a hand as he invited her into the boat chosen to take them across the lake. Sharmila accepted his hand, stepped into the boat, and then became self-conscious as she found herself still holding on to his fingers. She immediately let go and took a quick look at Alina. Usually nothing got past her daughter. Sharmila sighed, relieved that no one had noticed.

Alina had already found herself a comfortable spot on the cushions on the shikara. Surprising both her and Sharmila, George discussed details of the tour with the shikara boatman in a bizarre—but seemingly effective—combination of Urdu, Kashmiri, and Hindi.

“I admire your confidence in the languages,” Sharmila told George.

“Ah, well.” George blushed a bit. “I figured out that if I speak loudly and fast, most people think I know what the heck I’m saying. So now, based on my current knowledge of the Kashmiri language, we’re either going to end up at the most gorgeous floating garden in Kashmir, be offered leftovers for a meal, or the boatman is going to drop us at the Hyatt. Let’s see.”

“Charming,” Sharmila said as she noted how his eyes crinkled when he smiled. “You studied the languages here? I’m just guessing. With your degrees and all?”

“Well, yes, I’m fluent in Hindi and can get away with Urdu. And Kashmiri. Mostly. I’ve been known to use the wrong gender pronouns when I talk, and Wajid will tell you that I used to speak like I was a six-year-old when I first started. I learned Hindi when I fell in love with Indian art as an undergrad and decided to be as thorough as I could in my studies. Then I learned Urdu—well, some—when I came here on a Fulbright. I was a professor my whole life until now, after I retired early. I help Wajid when I can and do some freelance work.

“But enough about me—you must look over there. That’s the family of swans you saw yesterday. See, there’s a black swan there. Just one. It makes an appearance once in a while, just like a politician around voting time.”

The swans came close to greet the new visitors. “It’s almost like they’re welcoming us,” Sharmila marveled.

Alina had her phone out. “Look, Emilio, this is the lake. Yeah, yeah, I know it might still be partly frozen in early March, so Ma is now talking about April here and you know, that date … it isn’t negotiable. Yeah—I'm not really sure about this place, but you know Ma. Anyway, look at this—there are so many floating houseboats and—oh, my, look at that shikara, the lady is selling flowers." Alina's running commentary made George and Sharmila exchange a look. "So glad to hear that your nonna is better."

Alina turned the phone around and a very tired Emilio waved to everyone as Alina made quick intros. "I'm off to make her breakfast now," Emilio told her. "Listen, enjoy the trip with your mom. Nothing like going home to your roots, trust me. *Ti amo.*"

As the boat made its way towards the center of the lake, the sun began to warm the air further. They were grateful that the thin roof provided some shade.

George pointed. "Look at the reflection there in the water. Do you see the reflection of the white dome in these gorgeous blue waters? That is the Hazratbal Mosque, over there, on the north shore of the lake. It's one of the most magnificent structures here in Srinagar, and I think the world over. I will take you there for a visit. The name translates to *the respected place* and it truly *is* one of the most respected places here."

The ladies gazed in awe at the reflection. The shrine stood elegantly across the lake. The shikara boatman began to hum some new Bollywood tunes as he continued to paddle the boat and George went on.

"Take a look, ladies. That, over there, that is the Shankaracharya Temple on the hill there. In the distance. I'll take you there soon too. And that, in the far distance, that mountain—that's called Hari Parbat."

Sharmila gasped, coming to a realization. Vikram had told her about this view over and over again. Even though she had never been here, Sharmila had painted it from his words. The blue waters, the white temple set in the green hills, it was poetic in view and in the painting. It was hard for her to believe this was it in real life.

The shikara drifted on at a leisurely place.

"We are here now at Char Chinari," George announced as he gestured to a small island that housed Chinar trees with their glowing red leaves casting their shadows into the surrounding water. "It means the four sides. Look at the Chinar trees. They are lovely."

"I understand some of these trees are hundreds of years old," Sharmila said, mesmerized.

"Indeed. There is an awesome couplet that talks about the influence of the Chinar here. It is by Allama Iqbal.

Jis khaak ke zameer me hai aatish-e-chinar,

Mumkin nahi ki sard ho woh khaak-e-arjumand

"Alina, it means that it is impossible for the dust that carries the fire of the Chinar tree to cool down. The tree is said to be magical."

"The leaves do look like they're on fire," Alina agreed, and of course began to take pictures.

"There is history in every corner here. This island was built by a Mughal emperor. These trees, they can be found in all the parts of Kashmir. There is something very soothing about them—their majesty, their beauty. In April, their leaves will be green, and you can see a different beauty then." George stopped talking for one second and Sharmila took over.

"Yes, I painted a winter version of these. I called it 'Resilience and Hope.' These trees come back year after year, reminding us what strength means. It was one of the first things I learned to paint from Alina's father," Sharmila told him.

"You'll have to show me your paintings," George said. "I'd like to see them."

The boatman stepped into the conversation and explained that many movies had been shot near the Char Chinari. Then he began to sing a famous old song from one of the films. To Alina's surprise, her mother and George joined in.

"*Accha toh hum chaalte hain* ..." The boatman, Sharmila, and George began to passionately belt out the old Bollywood tune with varying degrees of tunefulness.

"You both seem totally into the whole Kashmir vibe," Alina remarked. "I wish my Hindi was as good as George's. But I know the line you're singing means 'Okay, I am leaving now.' Am I right?"

Sharmila nodded. "Yes, it was one of my favorites. Such an old tune."

The sun, which had been so bright a little while ago, disappeared behind the clouds. A chilly wind blew in their direction, bringing with it a few leaves that had fallen off the Chinar trees. Everyone shivered.

"Well, there is one more reason you're here in the middle of this lake as you plan for the wedding," George said to Alina. "One of the most honored traditions of Kashmir is the very fragrant kahwa, the tea that we were drinking when you met us."

"Yes, Vikram loved it," Sharmila said softly as the memory of her love flooded her mind. Vikram, she remembered, had often told her that his favorite kahwa was served at Ahmed Zindari's store. In fact, it was the subject of one of her paintings after she met him. She had painted his long, paint-stained fingers holding a white porcelain cup filled with tea. There was no kahwa in Jaipur, her hometown where she had met him, so she had painted the colors from his descriptions.

Vikram had told her, "Your art breathes, Sharmila. Your strokes are so fluid—strong and yet they have this feeling of being exposed, vulnerable." He often spoke of her paintings as though they were living creatures.

She'd replied, "I don't know about all that, but I do love the idea of painting the colors of my life … and soon, I hope, our life."

"Vikram?" George asked, and when Sharmila, lost in thought, didn't reply, he said, "I don't mean to pry. I'm sorry."

"Ma, Ma? George is asking you something."

"No, no, I *am* sorry," George said quickly. "It's none of my business."

Sharmila's voice quivered. "It's okay. Vikram was Alina's father. He was shot here in Kashmir during a rally of some sort, before she was born."

Sharmila paused, overwhelmed by a rush of memories from the arguments and subsequent estrangement from her parents.

"When I first met him, Vikram often talked about his childhood here. He *loved* the raad on the lake. I try hard to remember all that he said. But it's been decades now, and my memories are getting hazy." Sharmila wiped away the tiny tear that had started to form.

George hastily offered a white handkerchief. "I didn't mean to bring up any pain. I am so sorry to hear that about him. Kashmir has seen more than its share of senseless violence and so many lives have been lost. I am so sorry."

Alina was staring at the handkerchief. "What century are you both from? George, who carries one of *those* still? Come on, that is going to be the most ancient thing I'll see on this trip. A *handkerchief*."

The mood lightened. George smiled at Sharmila as she wiped her tears. She could smell his cologne on the fabric and hoped he wouldn't ask for it back.

"Anyhow, the raad, you mentioned," George said. "Yes, the raad are the floating gardens. There are still some lilies there, you see? We're a bit late in the season. But in any case, I brought you both here to meet Mustafa."

Just as George said this, a shikara pulled up near theirs. The boatman stood up and greeted George across the water as though they were old friends. His shikara was filled with bowls containing Kashmiri saffron, cinnamon, cloves, almonds, and rose petals, and he was holding a big pitcher of kahwa.

Alina squealed, "Oh my God. Wait, wait. I've heard of him. I've heard of this tea vendor selling tea in Kashmir from his shikara. Oh, he is so familiar … where did I see him … wait, I know."

"He was featured on *Food Stars of India*," Alina and George said at the same time. "Yes, I learned about him from Instagram," George added.

"Wait, *you're* on Instagram?" Alina asked George, incredulously.

"Why, of course. I'm not a Neanderthal. I mean, who *isn't* on Instagram?" George pushed his nose up in the air.

Alina looked at Sharmila, who blushed, and they all started laughing.

"I don't need Instagram or any of those social media things.

Look around. Who needs all that?" Sharmila said. "Anyway, do we get to be properly introduced to Mustafa?"

Before George could make up for his tardiness, the young man spoke up.

"Greetings and welcome to my home. I will serve you the best kahwa in Kashmir. It has special Kashmiri saffron and rose petals. I bring the tea to you. George here tells me you have a wedding coming up. I am happy to provide this service to all your guests. But first, you must taste the tea. Thank you, Mr. George. Give Wajid my regards. My wife tells me his ankle is hurt."

"How does everyone here know everyone?" Alina said.

"That is the beauty of these small places, you know. Once you are here, you are family," George said. "It's one of the reasons I live here now. It makes me feel like I am always home—you know, a place where everyone knows my name. Like *Cheers*."

Sharmila smiled at the reference to the TV show. Alina was clueless.

Mustafa poured the tea into tiny red paper cups and handed one to each of them. While Alina and George debated how exactly to sip the tea and whether the rose petals may or may not have added the purported magic, Sharmila put a hand over the side of the shikara, into the water.

"Vikram, I have done what I promised I would do," she whispered. "I have brought our daughter home. Do you feel us here? Are you here?" A white lily became entangled in her fingers, and she pulled it out of the water.

"Pamposh, Ma. That's a pamposh, right? Like the name of George's pretend palace," Alina said cheekily. "Don't you love these? So pretty."

"Yes, they are. I am so happy to see you smiling, Alina. And I must say that this tea is divine. So, the first task is done. We have tea. Now, what about all the other three hundred things we need for this wedding—we need a venue, a caterer, and …" Sharmila frowned as she began to count out loud all the things that needed to be done.

George put up a hand to stop her. "First rule of the valley is that you have to relax. All that you want will come to you. To us, in this case. Don't worry. I actually have a list of things to go over with you. We'll cover it all. For now, drink this tea, enjoy the lilies, and let me take you to the houseboats. Your guests can stay in houseboats here instead of typical run-of-the mill or *biscuits-cutter* hotels, as your wedding planner would have said. I'll show you the best ones here—they will accommodate your friends *and* take care of all their needs. Alina, you mentioned it will be a small wedding with just about thirty or so guests, right? The Sukoon is one of the best in the valley, in my opinion. It is a stunning houseboat."

Alina nodded. "The idea of houseboats sounds awesome."

"I will show you mine someday. I live on a small one," George said.

"That would be lovely!" Sharmila said. "I have never been in a houseboat. And yes, it *will* be a small group. I'm not sure how small at the moment."

Sharmila hoped that someone from her own family would attend, but she hadn't been able to reach her sister. *In this day and age*, she thought. Her sister routinely went into silent retreats, giving little or no notice to the family. Her parents had passed away about a year ago, without ever meeting Alina. Her sister had kept in touch, on and off. Over the last year, they had been talking a lot more and it had made Sharmila feel wonderful.

After bidding Mustafa farewell, George instructed the boatman to make a few rounds of specific areas of the lake that he loved. They made one more stop before heading to Sukoon.

They met Zarina, his favorite flower vendor on the lake.

George introduced Zarina and explained what was going on. "These ladies don't want to get flowers from a big shop or give big companies their money. You will take care of them in the spring, Zarina? This young lady wants local flowers for her wedding."

Zarina pulled out her phone in an instant. "Yes, yes, George, you know, I do this. Look at this, madam. My son and I make wedding decorations with wood and dried flowers, and we paint the dried leaves. You will have a wedding like no other. And, of course, if you have it in spring, you will have all kinds of tulips, daffodils, and daisies and more. But the money?" She looked concerned and turned to George.

He said easily, "Zarina, let them decide first. Don't worry."

Sharmila and Alina looked at the humble but eclectic designs that Zarina showed them.

"Ma, her designs are simple," Alina whispered. "What do you think? I do like them."

"See this, this is our Lilly Be Silly arrangement." Zarina showed them some more photos. Both Alina and Sharmila were impressed.

"Yes, see, I told you," George said. "She creates elaborate pieces of art with her flowers that are often playful and sweet. Trust me on this. She's the best in town."

"Thank you, Zarina. We will let you know our decision very

soon," Sharmila said, waving goodbye as Zarina's shikara pulled away.

George turned to the boatman. "Please turn the shikara around. We have to go to the other side."

As the boat turned, and the afternoon set in, the crowds on the lake diminished and tranquility returned.

Chapter 4

"Here we are at the Sukoon." George broke the quiet mood on the boat. "This can be the main houseboat for your guests. I texted the owner so he's expecting us. There he is. Come on in, let's step inside and I'll show you how to live on the water."

Sukoon sat majestically in this secluded part of the lake, looking at the snowcapped Pir Panjal Range A number of shikaras passed by filled with tourists, with vendors not far behind.

George told the shikara boatman to pull up to the entrance of Sukoon. Alina quickly jumped up and was on the houseboat, chatting up the owner.

"Ma, did you know this boat used to be called *Neil Armstrong*? They changed the name only a few years ago," Alina said as she took pictures of the boat.

"Yes, my father had named it that," the owner chimed in.

Sharmila stood up slowly and George offered her his hand again. She smiled at him, a bit shy at first, and then took it. "You have a delightful daughter, Sharmila," George said, guiding her onto the houseboat.

"I am blessed. She is spirited and has a mind of her own! She keeps me on my toes for sure," Sharmila said.

The dark wooden boat boasted a lavish interior that seamlessly blended modern luxury with age-old Kashmiri aesthetics. "Everything has character," Sharmila remarked.

"This is for you." The owner gave them both a light-blue shawl with Sukoon embroidered on it in pink. A soft pink border graced the edges of the shawl. "We give this as a welcome gift to all our guests."

"Thank you for this. It is most gracious of you." Sharmila was touched and grateful. She placed her own shawl in her bag and donned the new one.

"And now, George, let us show your guests the real magical place on the boat." The owner led the trio to the spot in the houseboat that usually clinched the deal in a minute—the sun terrace.

George, Alina, and Sharmila stood in the center of the terrace overlooking the striking lake.

In the distance, the raad, small floating gardens, danced on top of the lake. The mountains farther off gently hugged the horizon.

"I have always suspected the boat gets its name from this view," George said. "Sukoon means serenity."

Sharmila and Alina nodded.

Vendors on shikaras called out to them to buy daisies, marigolds, zinnias, lilies, eggplants, and lotus stems.

"Hello, sir, you should buy flowers for your lovely wife," a flower vendor called out to George. He smiled and waved her off.

Two waiters dressed in blue uniforms appeared with trays and offered them some saffron-rose tea and a Kashmiri tchot, an oven-baked bread.

"Take a bite. This is my favorite bread. It is pleasantly chewy on the inside," the owner said.

"Ooh, I love how this tastes. It's so different from other breads that I've tried," Alina said, then turned to the owner to ask him questions about the boat and how many people it could host.

"George tells me that there was some concern over the weather in the early spring? Let me assure you that this boat is well equipped for the Kashmiri cold. We typically don't open the houseboat until later, but if that is what you really want, we will make sure your guests are warm and cozy. Besides, if you are open to hosting the wedding in April, the weather will be glorious, and the valley will be at its best as that is the prime tulip season," the owner explained. Then he invited them for a late lunch and ushered them into the main dining salon.

The salon's walnut-paneled walls were engraved with many flowers, including lilies and roses. The cedar ceiling had a mesmerizing circular pattern. The chairs, the tables, and the daybeds all had ornate lattice wood frames.

"These rugs, see how colorful they are? They're called gabbas. I always found that name to be funny-sounding," George said. He looked up at the chandelier. "That's called a fanoos. I just love its light in the evening. When the lake is quiet and the sun sets, this particular fanoos just sparkles. Even the lake in the evening is something else—it looks like liquid gold."

"Ah, George, I am honored that you love my boat so much, and yes, we can't compete with Mother Nature." The owner grinned. "Now, today's lunch is a special treat for your guests. We are going to serve a nadur—basically, lotus stems in yogurt—

and then my favorite, haaq. That is greens with garlic and green chilles. And of course, several meat kebabs seasoned with saffron that my cook has made for you all. Here is another tidbit for you, Alina. October is saffron season in the valley so everything has an extra touch of saffron at the moment."

The large table in the center of the room boasted intricate carvings on the legs. The staff brought in food in silver-plated chafing dishes. Heady aromas of spices, freshly baked bread, and steamed rice quickly filled the air.

"Oh my God, Ma. You have got to try this rogan josh. It's even better than the one you make!" Alina exclaimed, tasting a large spoonful of the meat curry seasoned with cloves, bay leaves, and cinnamon.

"I am delighted you like this dish. We braise the meat in ghee and, of course, the red color is from our traditional Kashmiri red chili, and that aroma, yes, it is saffron," the owner said. "Please take your time and enjoy. This meal is meant to be savored, much like all the views around Dal Lake. I will join you in a bit." He left and the trio began to discuss all the different dishes.

Alina was impatient to see the rest of the boat. "You both can keep eating, I'm going to explore," she said and left.

Sharmila turned to George. "Til yesterday she didn't even want to be here. It makes me happy to see her learning about her father's hometown."

"What about you, Sharmila? Where are you from? Do I remember right—Jaipur?"

"Me, yes. I grew up in Jaipur. I think I spent most of my youth exploring the stepwells and palaces of Jaipur. I miss it. I haven't been back since before Alina was born." Sharmila suddenly remembered she had not yet heard from her sister and made a mental note to call her again and prayed that she would actually answer this time.

"Will you and Alina be visiting Jaipur? Has she seen your hometown?"

"No, not yet. I was hoping that after this visit she would want to do that. For this visit, I just want to show her, and I guess myself, all the beauty of Kashmir."

"Yes, I hope I can find you more places that she will like," George said.

"Do you have any children, George?" Sharmila asked, refilling her plate with nadur monje, crispy lotus stem fritters seasoned with fennel seeds.

"No, no. I wish I did. It would make life a bit sweeter." His voice was tinged with deep sadness.

"Yes, children *do* that. And your wife? I would love to meet her." Sharmila so wanted to see who was married to this marvelously handsome and smart man.

"Daneen. Here is her picture." George held out his phone and showed Sharmila. Daneen was dressed in a flowing red lehenga, a beautiful bridal floor-length skirt with a blouse, with golden embroidery. Her hands were covered in intricate henna patterns. He was seated by her side holding her hand.

"She is beautiful. And what a lovely name: Daneen."

Sharmila could feel the love in the photo.

Chapter 5

Four Years Earlier
George Washington University Hospital,
Washington, DC

"You're going to need surgery." The cardiologist showed the test results to George and Daneen as they sat opposite him in his office. "I'm afraid that this time, it's urgent. I'm going to get everything set up in the hospital this afternoon. I spoke with the cardiac surgeon before you came in. I'm not letting you out this time, Daneen. Now we have no choice. Your heart is in serious trouble."

Daneen held onto George's hand. "I don't want surgery. I don't want anyone cutting my chest open. I know I can take care of this in my own way. I will continue my meditation and my breathing practices."

"But Daneen—" George knew it was normally useless to argue with her. Once she made up her mind, even a miracle of God wasn't enough to make her change it. But this was one battle he was not prepared to lose.

The cardiologist's tone was firm. "Daneen, this isn't about

your meditation practice. We have always known that at some point you would need to have surgery. This isn't about any emotional trauma that can be healed through the mind—this is a real physical issue. There is a defect in the wall of your heart. We need to deal with it, and now. I have known you for many years and you have always done what you pleased. But this time, not just as your doctor, but as your friend, I am telling you, this is serious."

Daneen looked pleadingly at George. Her hands were shaking, and beads of sweat had formed around her face. Her hazel eyes scrunched and tears rolled down her cheeks. "George, I don't want to have surgery. I don't."

George held both her hands in his and tried to gently reassure her that the doctors would take good care of her. "Can we talk about this? Daneen, this isn't just your decision. It's *ours*. I don't want to lose you, my love. You are my life. Please, can we just discuss this? The surgeon they're recommending is the best in DC."

The doctor added, "He's right. Dr. Moskowitz is the best in town and he's here and in the hospital. We need to get you in to be prepped. He needs to run a few tests and then the surgery will be tomorrow morning. Daneen, this is a matter of life and death. There is no choice here, in my opinion. We have been over this for years. I warned you last year that—" He stopped as Daneen began to weep.

"Oh, my love, it will be okay. Please don't cry." George leaned in to console Daneen. "This is routine surgery these days. We can't *not* do this. It is your life, my darling. Our life. Yours and mine. I can't … we can't—" George's eyes filled with tears and he too began to weep.

The doctor said softly, "I know you don't believe in Western medicine, Daneen, and I've always supported you and respected your perspective. The herbs, the music therapy, your meditation practice, I think it has all contributed to your healthy life so far and kept your heart as strong as it could. But this can't be totally healed by alternative therapies. It's a physical defect that needs a physical intervention. I've always supported you, as long as I've known you. But please, we must get you admitted."

"Daneen, you've been having difficulty breathing," George reminded her. In the last few days she'd been lying in bed more often than not, totally exhausted. Even a few steps to the bathroom were hard on her.

"How much time do I have if I don't wish to do this?" Daneen asked quietly.

"Daneen, no." George knew his wife of twenty-five years well enough to know where this was heading.

The doctor replied, "I'm afraid I … well, at this point … with these test results …" He shook his head. "You're so *young*."

"No surgery. How much time do I have, doctor?"

"Your heart is not even functioning at fifteen percent. It may stop anytime. Even in a couple of days, I am afraid."

"I am the daughter of a hakim, a healer. I should be able to heal this. I have been able to do it all these years. At some point, my father did allow his patients to have surgery. But it wasn't often. And I—" Daneen was out of breath. She began to gasp for air.

"Please, Daneen. Listen to him. Listen to *me*," George pleaded. "Your heart is failing."

"I want to go home now. I will let you know by this evening how I wish to proceed."

The cardiologist looked at George. "I'm going to write a formal objection to you leaving here right now. But I can't stop you. I beg you to reconsider."

George understood. "It's okay, doctor. Please add it to your report. I'll call your office this evening."

"Try to make it this afternoon. *This* afternoon. Please."

For the first time in her life, Daneen used a wheelchair to get back to the car. She had refused it earlier that morning, but now she could barely stand.

Daneen fell asleep on the short ride home. George parked the car in their driveway and opened her door. She looked so frail and weak. He had been aware for weeks that she was eating minimally and getting tired easily. Each time he mentioned it, her response had always been the same.

"I've got this. I will be fine."

George reached in and picked her up in his arms. It startled him, again, how light she was to carry now.

I should have said something. I should have insisted she see the doctor earlier, he began to chide himself, but then she whispered his name, opened her eyes, and smiled at him.

"I want to rest. I am tired," she said.

He placed her on the bed, on top of her favorite purple satin sheets. "I love how these sheets are so soft and so cool," she said as soon as he laid her down. It was the same line, for twenty-five years now. It was one of Daneen's traits that he loved dearly—always grateful for everything around her. In his entire life, he had never seen her utter an ugly word about anything. Not even when they lost their newborn to SIDS. Daneen had only given thanks for the angel that blessed their lives for a mere month. But both of them had lost a crucial part of their souls when the baby, Tara, died.

"George, can you bring me her blanket?" It was almost as if she had read his mind.

George rushed to the closet. The soft yellow baby blanket was hanging next to her wedding dress. Daneen never put anything in storage. She always said looking at these things made her appreciate every single moment that she held precious.

"Here, my darling. My love. Now, can we please talk?" George gave her the blanket, then sat down by her bedside.

"I miss her every day, George. I miss her." Daneen looked tired but George couldn't help noticing her eyes. The agitation that he had seen at the doctor's office was gone. Daneen had an amazing ability to instantly calm her mind and her nerves, as if on demand.

He envied her. "You're so calm. I wish I could steady my energy on demand like you can. You, how do you do it?"

"Well, you can cook like a chef, and I can meditate like a yogi. We each have our own talents, right?" She laughed her trademark laugh, a giggle that always sounded like a happy jingle.

"Daneen, can we talk about what happened today? I've looked at the reports again. Please, my darling. Just this once." Even as he spoke, he hoped against hope that she would listen to him.

"Talk to me about the time we met, George. I just want to hear your voice … keep talking to me. I promise you, I will make a decision soon. For the moment, please talk to me."

"Let me bring you some water, and then we can talk." George rushed out of the room, less for the water and more to wipe the tears off his face. He wasn't going to let her see how weak he really was.

He returned moments later with a glass of warm water with a touch of mint and a slice of lemon, just as she always liked it. Her eyes were closed and her breathing was labored.

"Daneen? Daneen? Open your eyes. I have the water. We need to talk, my love," George gently placed his hand under her head to lift her up. She opened her eyes as he propped her up on the pillows. She took the glass of water, held it with both her hands and began to sip it slowly.

George sat as close to her as he could. "Okay, yes, which story would you like to hear? I think I know, but your wish is my command. So tell me." He rested one hand lightly on her arm and with the other he clutched the end of the baby blanket. This was his entire life. This was his *why*. This was everything that meant anything to him.

Daneen smiled feebly. "Our first kiss?"

"Hah. I knew you would ask for that. It still doesn't seem like it was nearly thirty years ago, Daneen. Let me see if I can remember it all. We were on our third date, right? Hiding from your brother Wajid and his friends?"

"Yes, we were hiding from the world. Remember how they were all angry? You, a white man, with their sister. They were furious that I would even speak to you."

"Yes, I remember. It was in the houseboat, right? The one that your grandfather wanted to gift you?"

"No, George. How—" Daneen looked at him with dismay. "You forgot? Wait, no, you didn't. You're teasing me."

"You are my dil, my heart. How could I forget anything? I

am teasing! I remember clearly: it was on the shikara. I remember I had to pay him five times the going rate. Three times the rate to take us to a secluded point on Dal Lake, and the two extra times for the fact that I was a foreigner. Do you remember his name?"

"How could I forget a man who called himself Jheelwala Jackson—the Michael Jackson of the lake."

"Yes, Jheelwala Jackson. He took us to the center of the lake. I still remember. It was cloudy, and rain threatened. He looked away when we cuddled. He had warned me to be decent. I still remember."

Daneen held out the water glass. George placed it on the nightstand. "You were slow to kiss me then, and you are slow to tell the story now. Get to the good part, my darling."

"And you were impatient then, and you are impatient now. I remember I leaned over to kiss you on your cheek. I will maintain to this day that it was you who turned your face towards mine, and that's how I ended up kissing your lips. I was so worried that Jheelwala Jackson would throw us into the water."

"And then, then you asked me to marry you and you promised me that you would love me forever," Daneen sighed. Her voice was down to a whisper, her breathing labored. "Do you remember the song, George? The song that Jheelwala Jackson sang?"

"Yes, of course. Aacha toh hum chalte hain ..." Tears rolled down George's cheeks as he murmured the words to the fun song about two lovers talking about leaving each other and promising to return to meet again soon. It was painful to remember the words now.

"I guess it will be our forever song now." Daneen's voice was barely audible.

"Daneen, please." George knew his pleading was futile. He wept openly now. She was who she was, and he knew she wasn't going to change her mind.

"I'm going to tell you a secret now, my love," she said. "It *was* me. That kiss? I *did* turn my face towards you. I was that impatient."

George smiled at his beloved bride, this woman who had been by his side for almost three decades. He knew her words meant only one thing.

She said, "Our forever will end soon now."

She died the next day, just as she had lived, with grace and dignity, on her own terms and in her own way.

A week later, with a little bit of encouragement from Wajid, George packed up his life in Washington and moved to Srinagar to live in the houseboat her grandfather owned, to be near the garden where she had wanted to be buried along with the baby blanket.

Daneen had come home, and in many ways, so had George.

Chapter 6

October 2022
Srinagar, Kashmir

George waited for Sharmila and Alina outside the hotel in his Jeep. He'd had to help Wajid that morning, so over the phone he had suggested the ladies go to Lal Chowk to do some shopping, offering to meet them at their hotel after.

"India's first prime minister unfurled the Indian flag in Lal Chowk in 1948 shortly after the independence of India," he told them. "And now to information you can actually use—you can do some casual clothes shopping there if you like. It warms my heart to see it filled with people again. This chowk has seen its share of political unrest, rallies, and more. But now, I love that life is back to usual here. Oh, and be sure to check out the clock tower in the chowk. Alina, you may want to take a photo there to show Emilio. It is a unique place filled with so much history."

Wajid's ankle seemed to be getting worse. George thought it worthwhile to get it checked again, and Wajid, sharing none of his sister's reluctance about Western medicine, had agreed.

Now as he waited in his Jeep, George thought of Daneen again. His memories had come flooding in when he'd shown Sharmila her photo the day before. It had taken him all night just to get his balance back.

It had been years since her death, and yet the memories were so fresh. Grief, George had learned, was a giving companion—sometimes, unrelentingly so. He clearly remembered the days after she passed.

"Wajid, I could have saved her. But I gave in to her stubbornness. It's my fault that she died," George had confessed to Wajid when he called to tell him that his dear sister had passed away.

"No, George. I know my sister well. We all knew her heart was weak. She often told me she was living on time borrowed from the universe, just to be with you. I think in the end, perhaps, she felt it was time to go. It is the only way to deal with this—make peace with it, dear friend. Or it will break you."

It took little convincing from Wajid for George to take early retirement and stay in Srinagar. The houseboat, owned by Wajid and Daneen's late grandfather, was the perfect sanctuary for his grief. He filled it with all her artwork. Daneen had been a brilliant textile artist. Designing patterns on cloth using silver and gold threads was her specialty. "Tilla work is my life. These patterns all tell a story," she would say as she crafted some of the most elegant embroidery George had ever seen. She taught her craft at a local community center in DC and had small exhibitions to sell her pieces. All the money she earned, she sent back to Wajid to donate to local Kashmiri charities.

After moving to Srinagar, George spent many a night on the

deck of the houseboat, drinking scotch and nursing his broken heart.

"George, hello." Alina's chirpy voice brought him back to the present. "Good afternoon. Where are we heading today? Also, what happened yesterday? Mom said you looked upset when you left Sukoon. Did something happen?"

"Hah. No, no, nothing like that. Something came up and I had to go. Did you all get anything fun while shopping in Lal Chowk?"

"Dude, define 'fun' here. The clock tower you mentioned was nice to see, but the rest was, you know, a crowded shopping area. My mother thinks shopping for wedding jewelry is fun. I really wanted to see a nightclub. This isn't exactly my idea of fun, or a place for a wedding or … well, you know," Alina said, looking rather frustrated.

"You're being a doll about it, I must say. Since I'm not a wedding planner, tell me, why does she want you to get married in early spring?"

"Oh that. Yeah, she and my dad were supposed to get married here on her birthday, at the beginning of April."

"Oh, I see. Well, April is the perfect time as it is the best season in Kashmir." George then changed to a softer tone. "You said 'supposed to get married'? What happened?"

"Yeah, so." Alina hesitated. "Ma was pregnant with me, and she and my dad wanted to get married *before* she had me. But … well, that never happened. And her parents disowned her because of the pregnancy."

"Oh?"

"She never married him or anyone else," Alina said softly. "My adorable Ma deserves so much more than what life has handed her. I see her happy here. Your stories have made her smile. I cannot tell you how happy that makes me. I told Emilio last night that if we have to be here, it's good we're here with you."

"You're a darling, Alina. I don't mean to pry, but why didn't they get married? What happened?" George was beginning to guess. It hadn't occurred to him until now that Vikram was killed before they married, but it was too late to back out of the conversation.

"I think my father came home here to tell his family about her. I don't really know what happened to him after that. I think he went missing and was presumed dead. In any case, that's the reason." Alina stopped for a minute, debating whether to continue. "I never knew my father, but I wish I did. Every Father's Day, I would imagine that he was there with me telling me how much he loved me. Thanks to my mom, I have heard wonderful stories about what a kind man he was. Today, I'm here because of my mom. And I *do* want to honor her wishes. But honestly, George, getting married in a country where I don't know anyone? It isn't easy."

George nodded. "I'm sorry, Alina, about your father. But, yes, I understand your hesitation. It's lovely of you to support your mom like this. But don't you think if you really, honestly, tell her that you don't want the wedding here, that she'll understand?"

"She's never asked anything of me. She has always given me everything. I am honestly warming up to this idea. It is funny that Mom was a rebel when she was young, but here she is being all traditional."

George nodded. "Well, I think that is enough deep conversation for one morning! I have a great day planned for you both. First, I'm going to take you to a special shrine that's very famous here. Then the rest of today is all about shopping. Your mom mentioned she wants you to buy your wedding dress here. Believe it or not, I know the best places here to buy wedding clothes. I guess I've traveled so much with Wajid, I didn't even know I knew this," George said, laughing. "Speaking of your mom, where is she?"

"Oh, she's coming. She said she had to talk to someone."

George saw Sharmila coming out the door, and for a moment the sight of her took his breath away. She was dressed in a stunning pink saree. Her hair, which had previously been in a stern bun, was now open and cascading down her shoulders. Her lipstick matched the color of her saree, and as she waved to him, he could see that her glass bangles matched too. The blue shawl from the houseboat was neatly folded over her arm.

"Good morning!" she called. "Sorry I'm late. I was just talking to the manager. Where are we headed today, George? We have so much to do for this wedding and don't even have a venue. Oh, and did I tell you that we decided to hire Zarina for the flowers? She sent Alina more pictures of her arrangements with tulips and won Alina over. And yes, the houseboat, Sukoon, too? Do they need a deposit?"

As they got into the Jeep, George looked at Sharmila. "Take a breath. It will all get done. You decide on everything first and then we can go to all these folks and confirm with deposits. It's at least five months away, right? So it will be fine. Don't worry."

George drove the Jeep onto the main road. The streets were already bustling with tourists, vendors, and schoolchildren. A few uniformed guards patrolled parts of the city as they drove through.

"George, is it even safe to have a wedding here? I mean … what about those guys?" Alina stared at the guards.

"Yes, yes, it's safe. I mean, I wouldn't go out in the middle of the *night* looking for trouble. I haven't had any issues since I've been here. They leave you alone as long as you don't go messing with them. That said, I'm glad I wasn't here years ago during the insurgency."

George drove quietly for the next few minutes as Sharmila and Alina peered out of the Jeep and took in the picturesque views of the valley—dotted with the armed guards. While most troops had cleared out of the main town, there were still a few scattered soldiers keeping the city safe.

"Where are we heading today? I got distracted with all there is to do," Sharmila said, brushing back her long hair fluttering in front of her face.

George turned the Jeep into a large parking lot. "Good timing on your question. This Islamic shrine, Khanqah-e-Molla, built by Sultan Sikandar, is one of the most revered in Kashmir. I want to show you something special. Come on."

On the banks of the Jhelum River, the shrine had survived for centuries. Its walls held prayers from lovers, families, and the distraught who came in to ask for blessings. The large mosque had a patio that welcomed them. Thousands of pigeons seemed to cover every open area. Several local ladies were throwing seeds to them. Sharmila could hear chants coming from all sides.

The interiors were adorned with antique chandeliers, the walls and pillars painted with colorful flowers in muted greens, reds, and yellows. Stylish calligraphy adorned the walls, spelling the word *Allah* in Urdu.

"Kashmiris take great pride in this shrine. It's not only one of the oldest, but I feel like it's one of the most welcoming. Even though it was built in memory of a Sufi saint who was instrumental in the spread of Islam in Kashmir, everyone is welcome here to come and pray and ask for divine help," George said, showing them various exterior features of the shrine.

There were separate entrances for men and women. Sharmila and Alina covered their heads with their shawls out of respect and entered the shrine. It was peaceful inside. Sounds of worship could be heard as women prayed in unison. They spent some time taking in the sacred ambiance. Sharmila admired the paintings of the flowers on the walls and the beautiful, green-painted interior. Both of them sat down on the elegant carpet in silence, listening to the women around them.

When they stepped back out, they saw George talking with an old Kashmiri man who hugged him and appeared to give him a blessing.

He told them, "That man is my wife's grand uncle. A lot of her family is still here. Did you like the shrine? It's so peaceful, isn't it?"

Sharmila said warmly, "Yes, and I am grateful you brought us here. I would love to come here one day and paint this in real life. What a beautiful and peaceful place. Every moment with you is increasing my love of Kashmir. I feel like a void is slowly being filled."

"Ma, you've got to show George your paintings," Alina said. "George, she has paintings of so many of the places you've taken us to, paintings that she made years ago. That's why some of these places look vaguely familiar. I've seen them in Ma's paintings." She looked expectantly at her mother.

"All right, here … George, take a look." Sharmila held out her phone.

George took the phone and sat down on the concrete patio, scrolling through photos of Sharmila's oil paintings. Paintings of the valley, the Char Chinar island, the mountain ranges, hands pouring the kahwa tea into cups, the white and pink pamposh flowers, the glorious views of sunrises over Dal Lake. He took his time and studied each painting.

"I feel like I may have seen some of this artwork. Did you ever have your art in an exhibition in DC?" he asked.

"Yes, I had a few showings at the National Portrait Gallery and also some at the Kennedy Center when they did events focused on India."

"At the Kennedy Center? In 2016? January? When they had all the chefs from India fly in for the Love of India event?"

"Yes, how did you know?"

"Daneen and I went to that one. I wanted to see all the famous jewels they had brought in from the Indian subcontinent in that exhibition, and I was one of the speakers. I'm certain we may have been there at the same time."

"It sure is a small world," Alina said.

"These are incredible," he said, taking one last look before handing Sharmila's phone back. "You're not just any painter. You are a gifted artist."

He went back into tour guide mode. "I brought you here to this shrine for a reason. Daneen learned the art of embroidery here. This place, while being a central point for worship, also encourages art and artists. She came here to learn her tilla work.

In fact, when she sold her work, she donated most of the sales money here to enable other young women to learn."

"How wonderful is that?" Sharmila said.

"Sharmila, I know this place will bless you, and your art too. Just as it had blessed Daneen and her work," George said.

They both went silent. Almost apologetically, Alina finally said, "Well, I hate to say it, but I'm starving. Do we know where we are going to eat lunch?" She stood up and straightened her shirt.

"Why yes," George answered. "Today we're going to sample the wazwan. I'll take you to my favorite restaurant downtown. You'll get a taste of the food to see what Kashmiri dishes you might want to serve at the wedding."

As they drove, the wind again played with Sharmila's long, flowing hair. George couldn't help but steal glances at her delicate features. Her elegance and grace were endearing. He watched how she delicately cleared the stray strands of hair from her face, and a warm feeling stirred within him. He wanted to reach out and brush the hair aside himself. Or was it that he wanted to hold her hand? The sudden pang of desire surprised him.

What in the hell is happening to me? In that moment, he found himself torn between the haunting memories of Daneen and the growing attraction, if he dared to call it that, he felt for Sharmila. He had vowed to shut the door to love, to keep his heart protected from any more pain, but her presence was beginning to breach the barriers he had erected so firmly.

As the Jeep continued along the winding roads, George stole another glance at Sharmila, who now seemed more at ease, as if she felt his gaze upon her but didn't mind it. He silently wondered how fate had intertwined their paths and wondered, *what if—*

"George, I fear we're keeping you from your family … your wife?" Sharmila couldn't help but ask.

"No, I meant to tell you yesterday. Daneen, my wife, passed away a few years ago," George said, keeping his eyes fixed on the road.

Sharmila was startled. "I'm so sorry. I was only concerned. I was, I am … I mean, I am so sorry."

"It's all right. It's been a few years now. That's why I came to stay here with Wajid."

"I truly am sorry. I did not know. Oh, and speaking of Wajid, how is he doing?" she asked, eager to change the topic. She placed one hand gently on her heart.

"He's learning to get around on crutches. He said he would try to join us for the wazwan. I can check with him."

"Oh, no worries, I was just wondering. Do you know how long the meal will take? I have an appointment this evening that I can't miss."

Alina asked from the back seat, "Who are we meeting, Ma?"

Sharmila turned around. "*We* aren't meeting anyone. I'm meeting the hotel manager I met earlier today in regards to holding a possible exhibition here for my paintings."

George wondered why Sharmila had just lied to her daughter. Earlier today, when she was late, he had in fact peeked into the hotel and seen Sharmila talking not to the hotel manager as she had told them, but to a uniformed police officer.

Something wasn't quite right.

Chapter 7

"Here we are. I hope Raahat is here." George parked the Jeep and jumped out like an excited child.

Sharmila and Alina looked around in anticipation. So far George had delivered on every promise he had made. They were in the heart of the downtown of Srinagar. The afternoon sun warmed the air, and the market was buzzing. Street food vendors selling everything from deep-fried bread topped with semolina halwa to walnut fudge filled the air with sweet, salty, delicious aromas.

"Who is Raahat?" Alina asked. "And where are we going for this meal? Everything here looks like street food. I mean … are you actually thinking street food for the wedding, George? Maybe that could be awesome—my friends would love it. But Emilio's Italian nonna may not like that idea."

"Follow me. You're going to be stunned when you see what I am going to show you," George said sweetly.

The lanes were tight with dusty pathways, bicycles parked at random spots, clothes hanging out on clothes lines to dry, mothers wearing traditional Indian outfits and chasing their tiny children, vendors on bicycles selling everything from knife-sharpening services to vegetables to footwear.

George was now already walking way ahead of them, rushing deep into one of the lanes. Alina and Sharmila followed, calling his name. He just raised his hand and signaled to them to keep following.

A few young children now ran alongside Alina and Sharmila, singing a local nursery rhyme, "Kokro Kokro," and making sounds like a chicken. Sharmila stopped for a moment and opened her purse.

"Ma, they're not begging, you can't give them money." Alina looked horrified.

"Is this how well you know me, Alina?" Sharmila's eyes twinkled as she pulled some pieces of chocolates from her purse, bent down, and handed them to the kids, who clapped and danced. One little boy gave Sharmila a kiss on her cheek. "The hotel staff was kind enough to find me some bars of my favorite chocolate. But now I guess I will need more."

Alina smiled. It had been a long time since she had seen her mother this happy.

Earlier in the morning, when she'd called her fiancé, she said, "Emilio, I'm telling you, it's like she's blossoming into a new person. She's always seemed content enough—steady, you know? But now she seems … well, she seems *happy.*"

Alina had also found herself feeling better and better about her Kashmiri wedding.

Emilio was understanding and delighted. He loved Sharmila and wanted to see her happy. "Focus your energy on enjoying the time with your mom and taking in the stories George is sharing about Kashmir. We don't really know why the universe is putting our wedding there. Let's focus on learning, on gaining a new perspective."

They walked faster to keep up with George. "Alina, I feel so bad that I asked about his wife. It's so sad that he's a widower," Sharmila said. Alina just nodded as she looked at the shops, the people, and the food vendors all around her.

"Do you think Dad grew up in this area?" she said suddenly.

"I think so. This was a part of where his family was from." Sharmila was a bit taken aback. This was the first time since they had arrived that Alina had shown any real interest in her father's birthplace.

"This area, it has a really warm vibe, Ma. Isn't that what you always say when a place feels friendly? This sort of has that, or maybe the sun is getting to me. In any case, where is our fearless guide? Do you see him?" Alina looked in the distance trying to see where George had gone.

Within a few moments they found George outside a small restaurant called RS Foods. He was waiting for them at the entrance.

"We take off our footwear outside as a sign of respect before we enter," he said, kicking off his shoes. He waited for the ladies to do the same, then showed them in.

"So why are we here? I am dying to know! You always seem to have something interesting up your sleeve," Alina said.

George beamed. "Well, young lady, I have a surprise for you. You see, typically the wazwan, the Kashmiri feast served at weddings, is prepared by a waza, a head chef from a family who migrated to Kashmir centuries ago. It includes around twenty dishes that they cook in large pots over wooden fires."

"Yes, I knew that," Sharmila said. "Is this an old waza's restaurant? I guess we're in for a treat then."

"Well, yes and no. Traditionally, wazas were all men. But

recently women are being included and cooking wazwan. So, Alina, my dear, for your lovely wedding, I thought we would bring some equality into the kitchen and have a woman chef make your wedding meal."

As though on cue, a well-dressed Kashmiri woman wearing a chef's jacket joined them in the entryway. "George, how wonderful to see you again. Are these the wedding guests?"

"Raahat. Yes, these are my friends, Sharmila and her daughter, Alina."

"Welcome. It will be my honor to serve you my version of the wazwan. I hope you will enjoy." Raahat's voice was gentle.

Alina had to admit, George certainly seemed to know Kashmir, but more importantly, he knew how to win her over.

"Please come in." Raahat guided them into the main dining room. Large red pillows and colorful carpets graced the room, for seating on the floor.

"Please wash your hands and make yourself comfortable. I will bring the food and explain to you all what you are eating."

Despite her objections to being in Kashmir and having the wedding in this unknown town, Alina found herself excited. The room was filled with aromas of saffron, ghee, and freshly cooked rice.

The trio sat down in one of the larger seating areas. Within minutes, Raahat returned with a large brass plate.

"We call this a trami. This brass plate will soon be filled with food, which we invite you all to share. You will eat with your hands, and the shared plate, well, it is custom, but I also believe that it ties us together in a bond. There is nothing like eating together—the food just tastes better with your fingers and with loved ones eating by your side."

Raahat piled fragrant white rice onto the center of the plate and topped it with mutton kebabs. "This dish is called tabak maaz. It is deep-fried meat," she said. "It is one of the first dishes you will be served. There is a lot more food coming, so I am just warning you, from experience, to pace yourself."

"It's like fried ribs, Alina. Once you eat this, you will never look at ribs the same way," George added with a wink.

Sharmila took a bite. "My goodness, this is so crispy on the outside and so tender inside. I can't wait to try the other dishes."

"Pace yourself, like she said. Raahat serves up to fifteen or sometimes even twenty-five dishes here for a single meal," George warned her.

"Oh, I'm fine. I think you both should see how much you are able to eat, you know, at your age," Alina giggled.

"I am ready, Raahat. Can they give me their order?" An older woman, her head wrapped in a golden scarf, appeared from the kitchen that was deep within the back part of the eatery.

"Yes, please come. Everyone, I would like to introduce you to my mother. George, you have met her, I know. But as you can imagine, I need to introduce her again."

"Yes, of course," George said, nodding as Raahat made the introductions. Her mother asked what everyone wanted to drink and was pleased to hear that this was to be a wedding feast.

"Oh, you will make a beautiful bride, child. You will bring great blessings to any family that you are a part of." She added a few sentences in Kashmiri and both Sharmila and Alina turned to George for a translation.

George told them, "She is the loveliest human I have ever met. Alina, she said a special blessing for you. She said, 'May your love be as pure as the snow, as refreshing as the rain and your bond be as strong as the roots of the old Chinars.' Now, please tell her what you want to drink."

As her mother disappeared into the kitchen, Raahat looked a little concerned.

"What is going on? Is everything okay?" Sharmila asked.

"Oh, yes," Raahat said. "My mother is losing her memory slowly, and to be honest, very painfully. I like to keep her engaged and she likes being here. The only thing is that she will not remember you all or your order. So please bear with me."

Alina was clearly touched by the love Raahat displayed for her mother. She was quick to get up to hug the young woman.

"We totally understand. Please know that this makes the meal even more special. Because now, each time she meets us, she'll bless us all again," Sharmila said.

Raahat began to bring out all her specialties, including traditional rista—mutton meatballs in red gravy—and rogan josh, a ghee-laden braised meat curry. Each dish was better than the last. Lamb cooked in a yogurt sauce, lamb chunks with fennel, lamb in milk, lamb roasted over coals—lamb, it seemed to Alina, cooked in over twenty ways. The humble potato cooked in yogurt tried its best to find a place, too. The meal was complemented with a walnut chutney, a spicy tomato chutney, and saffron rice. Raahat made several breads which, she informed the guests, were not typically part of a wazwan, but she enjoyed pairing each one of the dishes with a different style of bread. By now, the meal was only halfway through.

Raahat's mother came out with various drinks, none of which matched the order, as Raahat had predicted, but then sat down with them and explained to them with a gentle and kind tone some of the dishes.

At one point, Raahat's mother announced that she was almost seventy, and then insisted on feeding Alina a spoonful of lamb curry by her own hand, saying that it would be a big blessing for the child.

Sharmila wiped away tears. Alina had not had the blessing of having grandparents from either side, and now in this kind valley, love was just pouring in from all sides. It comforted Sharmila greatly that her daughter was starting to feel at home and comfortable in India.

Alina found herself enjoying not just the meal but also the stories that Raahat and her mother shared.

Raahat told them, "My father was a great waza, but he had no sons, just me. Everyone thought his art of cooking would die with him. But he made sure I learned all his secrets. It has been my savior. It was during the pandemic that I started my business. I had to make a living. My father died during that time, and I had no other way to earn. Slowly the local community began to support me. Now, even the owners of local hotels give me business. I still have a lot to learn. I am nowhere near the master he was, but I learn with every dish I make."

Sharmila asked, "Are there any other vegetarian dishes? The potatoes were just terrific, but I'm concerned. I know we will have a few guests who may not eat meat."

"Oh yes, we have haaq saag—the server will bring it now. It is our signature spinach dish with garlic. We do a few other vegetables, like lotus stem. The wazwan is quite meat-heavy, but I can add whatever you want."

One of the servers brought out the haaq saag and a bowl of onion chutney.

Raahat added a spoonful of the chutney to the trami, their shared plate "I should have served you this in the beginning. But better late than never. This is a dish that I have added to the wazwan. My father used to make his chutney spicy with Kashmiri chili, but I like mine a bit sweeter. Here, see what you think."

All three of them reached for it at the same time and started laughing when their hands came together.

Raahat said, "You see, this is what I love. The food brings us together, and the taste makes the memories stay in our minds forever."

It took another hour to finish the meal.

"Can I ask you a question, Raahat, if you don't mind?" Alina asked softly.

"Of course."

"Why is your place here so hidden? I'm checking on Google, and Instagram, but I don't see any mentions, any reviews. Why aren't you telling more people about this place? Your food is amazing. The fact that you're one of the first women to cook this type of food—I mean, everyone should know about this, right?"

Raahat looked at George and they both smiled knowingly.

"You see, what I am doing goes against centuries of tradition and culture. Not everyone accepts this. I have been told to stay in my place, so to speak, many times over. Vandalism, name calling, and all that horridness is something I had to get used to. But I decided that I will let my food speak for itself. Food doesn't taste better if one gender or another cooks it. Food tastes good when someone prepares it with love. I stay behind the scenes and let the food speak."

Alina felt her eyes sting and she blinked away a tear.

Raahat's mom suddenly interrupted them. "Raahat, where is your father? He needs to come and finish cleaning the stove in the kitchen. I am going home. Tell him to come home when he arrives."

"Yes, he is coming. Don't worry. I will send him to you as soon as he comes here," Raahat said. Sharmila placed a hand on Raahat's shoulder and gently squeezed it.

When Raahat's mother left, Alina asked her, "Sorry, I thought you said your father had passed away?"

"Yes, but I don't want to tell her that. I used to do that, but then each time she reacts as though it is the first time she has heard it and goes into a deep spiral, and then she forgets about an hour later. So now, I don't say anything."

Raahat brought their attention back to the food as she told them all the other dishes she could make if they selected her to cater the wedding.

"This was one of the best meals I've ever had," Sharmila declared. "I really hope that you will cater this wedding and, of course, bring your mother. She is so kind. It will be a small group of people, and we don't know where yet, but we will soon."

George stood up first. "Thank you, Raahat. I continue to learn from you. Not just your amazing food, but how kind you are to your mother. It can't be easy, I know, taking care of someone who cannot remember. If I can ever help, just call me, please."

Raahat thanked them. "It was so nice to meet you. I hope to

see you all again during your stay here. Please do let me know about the wedding." Raahat handed Alina a gold and red silk pouch. "This contains the heart of Kashmiri cooking."

Alina peered into the bag and found a packet of local saffron. "Thank you so much, Raahat. You are so kind."

When Sharmila tried to pay, Raahat wouldn't accept any money for the meal. "It is my pleasure to help your daughter discover the land of her father. George told me her papa was from here. It is the least we can do for a daughter of our land."

Sharmila looked at George as if to say, *Please help, we need to pay her.* Instead, George said, "We are so honored that you have given us this gift, Raahat."

Taking the cue from George, Sharmila realized that the exquisite moment wasn't merely about settling the bill. It was a testament to the embrace of heartfelt hospitality.

"I feel like this meal has transformed us from strangers into kindred spirits," she said. "Much like your saffron, Raahat. It has left an indelible mark of love in my spirit. Thank you, from the bottom of my heart."

With those words, full stomachs, and even fuller hearts, Sharmila and Alina left the restaurant to find George outside with his shoes already on.

"Where to now, George?" Alina asked. "My stomach is so full that I think I need a nap."

George laughed and told them he was going to take them to a newly opened store that specialized only in bangles—all kinds, he told them, from glass to lac to plastic to gold and silver. He had seen a write-up in the paper earlier that day, and Wajid had insisted that he take them there after the meal.

Suddenly the trio was greeted by a surprise. The neighborhood was up to mischief, and they were about to get caught in the middle. It started with a splash of ice-cold water soaking the back of George's shirt. He let out a yelp and turned around to see one of the little neighborhood kids grinning at him and holding a small red water balloon in hand.

"Mister. You are in our way. We are having a water battle, and you are on the enemy side," the little one declared, aiming the next water balloon at George. Before George could react, Alina sprang into action, playfully stepping in front of him.

"I will protect him. You'll have to get through me first," Alina called, her eyes dancing with amusement.

Sharmila found herself on the brink of becoming collateral damage in the impending balloon crossfire. Before anyone could let loose another projectile, a young voice piped up, "No, no. We can't hit her. She's the chocolate aunty. She'll be on our side."

Sharmila chuckled, her heart melting at the endearing title. "All right, all right, I'm on your side," she agreed gleefully.

With that, the battle lines were drawn. It was now Alina and George versus Sharmila and the pint-sized army of neighborhood kids, fueled by the chocolates she had given them and armed to the teeth with water balloons of various colors.

"This isn't fair," George protested as he and Alina took refuge behind a row of old, weathered Bajaj scooters parked on the street. "We have no ammunition."

Alina grinned mischievously, plucking an old hubcap from the street and holding it up like a shield. "Fear not, my friend. We shall rely on the power of imagination and resourcefulness."

The kids, undeterred by their opponents' lack of water

balloons, rallied together, their laughter filling the air as they planned their next move. Sharmila joined the fun, grabbing a discarded cardboard box to use as a makeshift shield.

"This isn't fair," George yelled again as the water balloons came in at them.

"Everything is fair in love and war," Sharmila shouted as the first balloon hit Alina on her arm and another one hit George on his head. They could hear Sharmila laughing and giggling and strategizing with the little kids on what to do next.

"Here, since they have an unfair advantage, I will give you both one, too." Raahat was standing behind them and handed George a water hose.

He stood up and turned it on and began to spray the kids. The war was forgotten as the kids came running towards him and began to clap and dance as George kept on spraying water on them. Alina joined in too and laughed at the sweetness of the moment. She turned and grabbed the hose from George and began to spray him and her mom. Sharmila tried to shield herself with her hands, but now there was more than one hose. Raahat had joined in.

The noise attracted the attention of many of the neighbors, who all came out to see what the commotion was about and take part.

Sharmila twirled to avoid the oncoming stream of water and her eyes locked onto George's. The electric charge between them was undeniable.

Her foot slipped on the wet ground and for a heartbeat, she teetered on the edge of a fall. In that heartbeat, George was there, swift as the breeze, wrapping his strong arm around her waist.

His touch sent shivers through her. In his embrace, she felt safe, but her heart raced wildly as his other arm slipped behind her legs, lifting her effortlessly from the ground.

As Alina and Raahat joined forces, spraying them both with a symphony of water, Sharmila and George were drenched, their clothes clinging to their bodies like a second skin. But the sensation of wet fabric against their skin was nothing compared to their sudden and unexpected closeness to one another. As they continued to look at each other, the outside world faded away and they could barely hear the children or feel the water.

Sharmila instinctively nestled her head against George's shoulder, her arms gracefully finding their way around his neck. Their breaths became synchronized, and they could feel each other's heartbeat quicken. Their dance in the spray of water was a dance of restraint and desire, a subtle revelation of feelings neither was ready to put into words.

"We won, we won!" the kids were shouting.

Self-consciously, George put Sharmila down. She turned away and joined the kids in their chant.

The war had ended.

"Let's go sit in the sun to dry off," Alina said, walking towards a garden she had seen on her way in. George and Sharmila followed, very conscious of the effect of the physical closeness they had just experienced.

As they sat in the large sunny garden, George asked them if they wanted to meet Daneen.

"Meet Daneen? Yes, yes … why not?" Alina mumbled and looked to her mom for some clarification. Sharmila was confused and wondered if he had felt bad or guilty about picking her up earlier and so was now thinking of Daneen.

He said, "I don't mean to bring this up suddenly. It has been on my mind. Since I have told her about you, it is only fair that you meet her. We can go there after the bangle store."

With that, they made their way to the new bangle shop, where Alina purchased several dozen glass bangles. Sharmila was distracted with the prospect of "meeting" Daneen and what that might mean.

The shopping was done.

"Come on now, she's very close by," George said as they left the shop.

Within five minutes, they found themselves walking past the Hazratbal shrine and on to a garden filled with small green bushes. There was a tiny pond in the center of the garden with a fountain that was barely working.

Alina realized it was a cemetery.

Chapter 8

Sharmila tossed and turned that entire night. The mingling of the dance in the water along with the trip to the cemetery was all confusing, and her mind was filled with hope and expectation and refusal and chiding.

George had introduced her and Alina to Daneen's well-tended grave at the cemetery. At the gravestone, he placed red roses that he had purchased from a young girl at the gate and said softly, "I never thought I would see the day that I smile again, yet here I am. I know you'd want me to be okay."

Alina looked at her mother to see Sharmila wiping away a tear. It had been an emotional day with Raahat and her mother, and now, meeting Daneen in this way. Alina reached over and placed her hand on George, who was on bended knee by Daneen's grave.

His eyes still on the gravestone, George said, "Daneen, this is Alina. She is like a spark of joy personified. She is going to study to become a nurse, Daneen. I told you she is getting married, right? I spoke to him on the phone. What a nice young man. Emilio is studying law. Do you remember that I told you I am their tour guide? Yes, me. I guess this is my working retirement. And this, this is Sharmila. She is a talented artist. In fact, I think you and I may have even seen her work . . ." He became quiet.

Alina sat by George and held his hand. Sharmila began to pluck some of the petals from the red roses and spread them all over the grave.

Sharmila said, "Even though we never met, Daneen, I love that your memory has brought all of us here together." Sharmila placed her hand on George's shoulder. He reached up and squeezed it gently.

With that, they said goodbye to Daneen and left.

Sharmila had often pondered whether anyone else experienced the ache of losing a companion as intensely as she did. Her time with Vikram had been incredibly brief—barely eighteen months—yet now she almost felt a pang of guilt for harboring sadness as she looked at George.

"I can't imagine losing someone whom you've loved and lived with for an entire lifetime," she'd said as they left the cemetery.

"I look at my life with her as a blessing. Maybe that's the price one pays for love? Although it seems cruel to me that loving should have a price," he replied.

That response kept her awake. Should love have a price to pay? That *did* seem rather cruel. In his life, and in so many ways, her own.

She was up at dawn and dealing with the restlessness the only way she knew how—she painted. Sharmila was glad she had purchased some small blank canvases and a set of paints. She had her set of brushes, and in her painting bag, she always kept the brush that Vikram had given her decades ago. It was the only thing of his she owned.

Sharmila set up the canvas on a small table by the window.

She could see the Jhelum River in the distance and the sun rising over the top of the mountains. It was foggy outside, but the sun was doing its best to beat out the mist.

Sharmila began to paint the shy dawn with gentle brushstrokes. Yellow, orange, red—it seemed the colors poured from her soul more than her brush, each stroke bolder than the last one. As the sunrise unfurled, her brush became even bolder, gaining intensity that echoed the rising sun. She had always painted the valley from what Vikram had told her about Kashmir. It seemed surreal to be painting the scene while being there in person. She realized she viewed the valley differently from George. He loved it; she was in awe of it. He felt at home in it, and she felt welcomed. It was always so familiar to him, yet she felt surprised at each turn. She wondered if Vikram had ever seen the sunrise over the Jhelum in October. Had George?

The small painting was complete, barring one thing. She needed to sign it.

She inscribed her artwork, as she had for decades, with a single word, Rumshaya. This was an homage to the enigmatic figure Shams, who inspired the great Rumi himself. She never signed her true name, treasuring her privacy deeply. This silent tribute brought her profound comfort and was her way of connecting with and honoring two of her greatest spiritual teachers.

She hoped this painting, like her others, would offer the viewer serenity and fulfillment.

She stared at Rumshaya. She intended it as a heartfelt blessing upon the canvas and anyone who beheld, cherished, or took it into their lives.

She wondered what George would think of her art. He had

seen the photos of it earlier at the shrine and said he was impressed, but she was worried he was just being polite. Then her anxious mind did what it did best—it ran in several conflicting directions. She was here to plan for Alina's wedding, and Sharmila knew that was the right thing to do, yet found herself thinking of George constantly.

Alina had been more than accommodating about visiting Srinagar, even though Sharmila knew that her daughter's heart wasn't fully in it. Sharmila understood and at moments felt bad.

Sharmila had confided to George the day before, "Maybe I *am* being silly bringing her here. Maybe she's right. We should go back to DC. After all, Emilio's family is there. I just wanted to connect her with the land of her father. Maybe there's no need to have even a token wedding here?"

"Give it time. She will connect with Kashmir soon. It always happens. This place has that pull and she has roots here. Just give it time," George said.

Sharmila began to clean her brushes and put them away.

"Hi, Ma. You're up early," Alina said groggily from her bed. "Wow, that sunrise painting. It's so lovely. Dare I say even—cheerful?" She yawned.

"Good morning, my love." Sharmila often still saw Alina as a baby and had to remind herself that this was a fully grown young woman with her own mind and path. "I'm glad you're up. We're heading to Qayaam Gah—it's a private resort on top of that hill you can see from here. It's owned by the same man who owns Sukoon. George mentioned that they have Sufi-inspired rooms and a glorious heated outdoor pool and outdoor fire pits and more. We could easily host your wedding there."

Alina put the covers over her face. "Mom," she said. "Am I a terrible person if I say I don't want to go? We've been going, going, going since we got here. I'd really like a day to sit by the pool and read. Plus it's Emilio's brother's birthday, and our friends are doing a video call this morning and I don't want to miss it. Can you just go without me? I trust your judgment."

Sharmila, putting away her brushes, opened her mouth to protest. But then the idea of spending the day alone with George made her grin. She enjoyed his running commentary on literally everything. She loved that he was so consumed by his love of everything Indian. She reckoned he knew more about India than her and Alina combined. He knew every corner of Srinagar and adored it. From the difficult political history to the majestic scenic beauty, from the roadside food vendors to the elaborate wazwan, he seemed to know and love it all equally. His childlike enthusiasm for Kashmir was pure joy. It was so easy to get caught up in his optimism and fun. He made her want to be here, to laugh, to marvel at all the natural gifts the universe had endowed upon this valley.

But within a few seconds, her well-practiced guilt-tripping set in. "Alina, please, why don't you come? It's for *your* wedding, after all. Don't you want to see where it might be?"

"Not today."

Sharmila sighed. She knew not to push *too* hard. "All right, lovely, I will go look and take pictures. You have a beautiful day and tell Emilio I said hello. Remind him to send his measurements so we can get his outfit ready. I think he will look smashing in a sherwani. Those tunics these days are just as ornate as bridal lehengas."

Alina gave her mother a thumbs-up from under the sheets.

Sharmila got dressed quickly. This time she chose a white salwar kameez, a long tunic with pants, and matched it with a warm, dark purple shawl. She noticed herself taking a few extra moments to make sure she looked good. As she brushed her hair, she chided herself. *You are too old for this, woman. Stop it. Who knows, he may already have someone.*

The breakfast was typical of those served in five-star hotels in India. Strawberries, papaya, apples, oranges, freshly baked breads, and loads of Western-style egg dishes. Sharmila opted for a cheese omelet and was about to sit down to eat when she noticed the police inspector she had spoken to the day before out in the hotel lobby. She placed her plate on the table and went out to meet him.

"Any news?" she asked, her eagerness showing clearly. "Anything at all?"

"I am so sorry, Madam. I did not want to give you this news on the telephone. I have tried but it seems there are no records. The court that hosted the files was vandalized a few years ago and there is no paperwork. I have spoken to some of the neighbors, but I am afraid that this may be a dead end."

Sharmila thanked him for his time. In her heart of hearts, she held very little hope that she would be able to find what she was looking for. The inspector had been reluctant to even talk to her, but when he came to know that she was from a Jaipur royal family, he offered to do it as a favor. She had suggested money for his troubles, but he wouldn't accept it. The man had integrity.

"I am so sorry, Madam. If something does come up, I will let you know. How much longer are you here?"

Another week or so was her defeated response.

As he left, she saw George coming in. He was carrying a large, ornately embroidered golden silk bag.

"Good morning. Are we ready to head out? This is for Alina. She made quite an impression on Raahat. Raahat sent this over—it's filled with Kashmiri red chilies, her homemade walnut chutney and several different proposed wedding menus. She thought Alina would like to discuss the possible menus with her fiancé." George handed over the bag. He stopped for a moment, saw the look on Sharmila's face, and added, "What's wrong? You look upset. Where is Alina? Is everything okay?"

"No, it's nothing. I'll go drop this in the room. Alina isn't joining us today. I don't know, maybe this is all a mistake? I'm wondering if I should just cancel. I don't know about the resort. I am just worried now ..."

George smiled. "You really know how to worry. Is this also an art form that you are perfecting? Please don't worry." His voice was calming, and he paused as he considered their options. "Well, we can postpone Qayaam Gah until the young lady is ready, and I'll take you somewhere else today. While you're here, you should at least enjoy all that this city has to offer. We've barely scratched the surface of Srinagar." He thought for a moment, then snapped his fingers. "I promised you Shankaracharya Temple, but we never made it there. How about now?"

His smile, his demeanor, and his offer all made Sharmila smile, and it took little more to convince her to go with him. She found herself hurrying back to the room to drop the bag and then get back to him. *I am behaving like a hormonal teenager*, she admitted. *But oh, does it feel so good.*

George realized that he had been giving her a running commentary on everything under the sun after they had left the hotel. She had been happy to listen and loved hearing his voice.

"I'm usually a man of few words, but when I'm with you, I find myself wanting to talk about everything. I do apologize if I have been talking nonstop."

"Maybe we're filling the gaps in our hearts with these stories, one garden, one monument, one sight at a time?" Sharmila said.

George nodded. "It is one of the reasons I love being here. When I go with Wajid on his tours, and I see people becoming happy as they learn about the valley and all its secrets, it's what keeps me alive."

"So, you've only shared public information with me. What are the *secrets* of the valley, George?" Sharmila teased him.

"When the moment is right, I will tell you the secrets, too. Look there, see that place? That is the shop that sells groom's clothes. Remind me to bring you all back here."

The drive to the temple took less than twenty minutes.

George explained as he stopped the car, "Due to some new rules and regulations, we can't park near the temple. So, I'm glad to see you wearing flats—it's going to be a long walk. We'll have to climb over 200 steps to get to the top." He took a large backpack out of the rear seat.

As they began to walk towards the temple, George apologized that she would need to take a different way in, as the lines for men and women were separate. At the security gate they parted ways for a few moments.

As soon as they arrived at the base of the temple, Sharmila exclaimed, "I recognize this temple!"

George started laughing. "Is there anything that Vikram *didn't* tell you about? I'm trying my best to surprise you with something new on this trip."

"Actually, if he did mention this temple, I don't recall it. It's been so many years. Since I didn't make a painting of it, I'm guessing he didn't tell me. I only recall this from an old Bollywood movie—a Rajesh Khanna movie, if I remember correctly. This is the main Shiv temple, right? Yes, the other day with you on Dal Lake—you pointed it out to us, do you remember?"

Before George could answer, an older couple stopped next to them and the gentleman said, "Yes, 'Jai Shiv Shankar.' The song lyrics and the praise to Lord Shiva always holds true."

They all smiled. "Yes, that is the song," Sharmila said. "It is so old. I can't even remember which year now. Maybe early seventies? I was a toddler. But that song is evergreen." Sharmila thanked the couple and she and George began to climb up the steep stairs.

"This is the oldest temple in Kashmir and highly regarded," George told her. "My favorite part is the views at the top. I don't know how much we will be able to see though. Maybe we'll be okay if the fog has lifted."

The two of them continued on. George didn't complain, but Sharmila made a few comments about running out of breath. Passersby chanted prayers, singing about the glories and blessings of Lord Shiva, and encouraged each other to keep on going. Young kids ran up the stairs effortlessly. As the climb continued, the chants increased and the sheer joy the devotees felt was palpable.

George's commentary on the temple didn't stop all the way

up. "There is a myth here that says that Jesus visited this temple. But you know, if you say that out loud, it will cause an uproar. I just want to find someone who can prove or disprove it, you know? A myth is just that—a myth. This one says that all God is one. So I don't get the point of the protests sometimes."

Once they reached the top, both of them sat down on one of the stone ledges to catch their breath. An older Kashmiri woman approached them and said, "You are a lovely couple. Orzo the burkoth."

George began to laugh hysterically but Sharmila was puzzled, as she spoke Hindi but not Kashmiri. "What, what? What did she say? Why didn't you tell her we aren't a couple?"

"Sharmila, she said, 'May you always be blessed with flexible knees.' I am not going to give that blessing away. I need it." He continued to laugh.

Sharmila laughed. "I will take that blessing any day too!"

They went into the main sanctum of the temple to offer their prayers. The radiant yellow room had a magnificent, several-foot-high Shiv lingam—a unique divine ellipsoid stone—in the center of the room with the figure of a large snake surrounding it. The energy inside was vibrant as chants reverberated loudly, incense filled the air, and devotees sang the praises of Lord Shiva. The devotees offered milk, fruits, and flowers during the prayers.

When they came out of the prayer room, Sharmila was smitten by the views of the valley. Despite the slight fog, the lake glimmered in the light. Shikaras and houseboats filled the lake as the mountains stood guard around it. There were breathtaking views of lush green valleys and the houses nestled in the city of Srinagar.

"I can't imagine a place that's more divine than this. I can see snow. Look over there—it looks like a lot of snow on the mountain top. I guess it's that time of year soon," Sharmila said.

George stood behind her, taking pictures of her against the majestic mountain backdrop. Then he moved closer to show her the photos. Sharmila felt the heat of his body behind her, ever so slightly. He said, "This would be a great scene to paint, right?"

Sharmila nodded and pulled out her phone. "I thought you might like to see some more of my paintings. I hope that isn't too presumptuous."

"Sure, of course, but first I've got a surprise." George asked her to sit on a ledge overlooking the valley. He opened the backpack, took out a small tablecloth, and placed it in front of Sharmila. "Raahat sent that gift for Alina, but she sent something for you too." He took out various vegetarian samosas, a flask of hot tea, onion chutney, walnut chutney, and a few potato-stuffed wheat paranthas.

"This is lovely. I am so touched. You knew we would be coming here? What about Qayaam Gah?"

"Well, to be honest, Raahat packed the picnic for the three of us. I told her we were going to Qayaam Gah, but she mentioned that I should take you all by Nigeen Lake first as a bit of a detour. She thought you might enjoy the tranquility of that lake as it is a bit more peaceful than all the other spots in Srinagar. We never made it there, but I still think we can savor the meal here."

He took Sharmila's phone and began to scroll through the photos of her paintings. There were many scenic paintings of places she had visited, and a few of Kashmir landmarks that he recognized. He was mesmerized by the theme of the majority of the paintings: a woman alone in almost all of them, with flowing dark hair, flowing clothes, bejeweled and looking in the distance as though looking for a path, a way forward or onward, or a release.

"Sharmila, your adept utilization of a recurring motif—the solitary woman—evokes a sense of introspection and solitude. It draws me into each painting. The flowing dark, the red attire, the traditional Indian jewels on her. Such grace and fluidity."

Sharmila burst out laughing.

"What? Did I say something wrong?" George looked hurt.

"No, no. This is the first time I've seen the side of Dr. George the professor. Since I met you, you have never spoken so formally. Right now, I get this feeling that I'm going to be graded on my paintings."

"Hah. Fair enough. In that case, let me be a little more professorial, especially since it's making you laugh. The symbolism you've infused into these pieces is thought-provoking. The woman's bejeweled appearance could be seen as a representation of inner riches, while her gaze into the distance introduces an air of mystery, prompting us to ponder her aspirations and yearnings," he said seriously, trying to keep the smile off his face.

"That sounds like an A grade, professor," she said, grinning.

"Ah, let me go on then. I love your interplay of light and shadow. Like here, it highlights her form. However, I wonder, is the woman always alone in every painting? Is it reflective of an emotional journey? Can the journey change? Take detours?"

Sharmila's smile changed to a contemplative look. "Well, as you may have guessed, these are self-portraits. I guess those are the moments that I found solace on canvas. I love that you are reminding me about the potential stories within the canvas. I guess I never thought of her being anything but alone."

"Well, my dear student of the moment, you get your A+ grade. Let's toast with some tea," he said, lightening the mood as only he could.

"I will drink to that."

"I am curious though. Your signature on these. Why do you sign them Rumshaya? Is there a special significance?"

Sharmila explained who Rumi and Shams were, and how she came up with the name, adding that it was her quiet hope, a wish for her paintings to radiate peace and resonate with those who encountered them.

"I have to say, your paintings reflect an authenticity that's hard to come by these days. It's something I admire in your art and in you," he said. "I see the energy in them. It's *you*. I don't know how I know, I just ... see *you*."

Sharmila felt her chest get warm and hoped she wasn't blushing too obviously. No one had ever made such a personal connection between her and her work. *How nice it was to feel seen. No, how nice it was to* be *seen after all these years.*

For a few minutes they sat quietly in the sacred environment overlooking the peaceful valley and ate the snacks and drank tea. A young girl came up to Sharmila and tugged at her shawl. Sharmila smiled at the child and offered her a samosa. The child's mother came running up to apologize for the child intruding, but Sharmila was pleased and began to talk about the joys of having daughters.

George took the moment to look through more of Sharmila's paintings.

"You are still studying them, George. Now you are making me nervous. Are you planning to grade them again?" she asked, as she finished eating the last samosa, and the mother and child left.

"Nope. There is something else that I want to do." George told her he was going to set her up with an Instagram account. The world needed to see her images outside of the infrequent exhibitions where she showcased her work. Sharmila couldn't believe she was saying yes, but he convinced her.

The first image he loaded on was the painting he loved the most: an elegant woman, dressed in her wedding finery, dancing with abandon, her arms waving in the air as though inviting love in for the first time. Or perhaps again.

Sharmila was thrilled. That was her favorite painting as well.

The two began their descent to the base of the temple, talking about the blessed energy of the place, her art, her new Instagram account, and of course, the upcoming wedding. They were so engrossed that they didn't see the crowd that had gathered at the bottom of the steps.

"Looks like a flash mob," someone in the crowd said.

George and Sharmila hurried to the side of the steps and found a place to watch.

Young men and women came from all sides and joined in and began to dance to a combination of "Mujh Se Shaadi Karoge" (Will You Marry Me) and "Jai Shiv Shankar" (Praise to the Lord Shankar). Everyone around started to clap and cheer on the dancers. As the music began to reach a crescendo, a young man stepped forward and proposed to the lead dancer. The dancer looked shocked. It was clear she thought they were there for someone else's proposal. She began to cry and accepted the ring being offered. With a few hugs, and some cheers from the crowd, the dancing continued.

One of the dancers reached out and pulled George in. Another did the same to Sharmila. Both of them danced, laughing and giggling. George looked at her and tried to imagine what she would look like in real life as a bride—but immediately stopped himself.

After Daneen died, he had fallen into a deep despair. On one of his worst days, he had gone to a fortune teller on the streets of Srinagar. The woman told him that he would never find love again. It had all but destroyed him.

Yet here he was, totally in awe of this ethereal woman who had stirred emotions he never thought he would feel.

Chapter 9

"He's here, let's go," Sharmila called out to Alina, who was just finishing her shower. "He's never even a minute late. Actually, today he's fifteen minutes early. I think he said that Wajid would join us for a bit. I hope his foot is healed now."

"Ma, for once, can you stop worrying, please?" Alina yelled from the shower.

Sharmila had spent the early part of the morning painting another canvas. This time she attempted to capture the view from the Shankaracharya Temple. She found herself wanting to add an image of herself and George seated on the ledge, watching the sun. Then she thought better of it and painted just the view with the focus being on the valley. She added a fleeting image of herself sitting alone on the edge as though she were waiting for permission. *For what? From whom?*

"Alina, yesterday George graded me on my paintings. And he loved them. Even the ones that you think are sad …" Sharmila appeared more to be talking to the canvas than to Alina.

"Nice, Ma. This painting looks good. Kashmir clearly suits you. You know, I think this is turning out to be a fun trip after all." Alina's phone buzzed, stealing her attention. She wandered off to the other side of the room and buried her nose in the screen.

"Come on, Alina. We should go. Today won't be a long day. We're just going to shop for some traditional Kashmiri pashmina shawls." Sharmila packed away her brushes for the day. She looked at the canvas and smiled as the memory of the flash mob came back. "I must show you this video, Alina. Yesterday there was a group of youngsters about your age dancing, and here, here, see this?" Sharmila held out her phone and Alina came over to watch the video.

"Umm, there's more of George here than the flash mob, Ma. He's all you focused on."

"Oh, how silly of me. I actually danced with them as well, but there is no video of that, thank God." Sharmila self-consciously took her phone back and wondered how much truth there was in Alina's statement.

As they walked through the hotel lobby to meet George, Sharmila found herself feeling pure joy. She had to admit, it felt good. And more importantly, it felt easy and safe. Nothing about him was difficult. His easygoing manner was addictive.

"Good morning, ladies. Today, we'll be doing my least favorite thing—shawl shopping. To me, it is like watching paint dry. So we'll have to do one thing that I love to make up for it. I'm going to cook you both dinner," George told them.

"That sounds terrific, right, Alina?" Sharmila said. But Alina was on her way over to the concierge desk to talk about a sign in the lobby for a Taylor Swift–related event for that evening.

"Hold on, I am coming back," she called out.

"Alina, Alina—" Sharmila was clearly annoyed.

George said, "Oh, let her be. I'm sure she's looking for something to do that doesn't involve her mother or an old man like me."

Alina joined the two of them in the Jeep. "I may not be able to come tonight. They're going to text me if there's an extra ticket available for this Taylor Swift concert."

Sharmila turned around. "Wait, Taylor Swift is in Kashmir? That doesn't seem possible. There would be hordes of people here and signs and more if that were happening."

Alina explained that the hotel was putting on a show to celebrate a new record by the star and a local band would be playing her music in the ballroom with dinner and, of course, dancing.

While Sharmila asked a few more questions about the evening event, George noticed in the rearview mirror that Alina looked out of sorts as she answered her mother, and she kept looking at her phone.

His phone rang and he answered. It was a call from a possible resort for the wedding, and from what Sharmila could tell, he had already finalized the three they wanted to look at.

"You could easily be a wedding planner. This comes naturally to you," she teased him.

"Me? Ah, poor Mr. Rami—I don't mean to take away his business. This is just for you. Talking with Alina reminds me of the US, and I have to admit, I miss being there sometimes."

"Yeah, whatever," Alina said, looking out into the distance.

George looked over at Sharmila and raised his eyebrows as if to ask, *What is wrong?*

"Emilio," mouthed Sharmila.

"Lovers' tiff?" George mouthed back and Sharmila nodded.

Within minutes, they arrived at a pashmina shop on a large shikara moored on Dal Lake. They made their way onto the bright red boat and were met by the owner, Abdul Shaikh.

"I thought Wajid was joining us today, George?" Alina asked as they entered the main showroom.

"He was, but I think his ankle began to hurt again this morning, so his wife decided that he shouldn't. I think he wants to stay married, so the decision was obvious," he said with a wink.

The large room had white floor-to-ceiling shelves filled with colorful shawls. Four salesmen were sitting at various points in front of the shelves.

"Please come in and have a seat. Can we offer you some kahwa? Or coffee?" Mr. Shaikh asked the guests.

Alina answered immediately. "Coffee, please. I've tried kahwa and it's great, but coffee *really* sounds good right now."

Once they were settled, she turned to Mr. Shaikh. "So tell me, what's the big deal with these shawls? Everyone says they're so special. Is it all just good marketing?"

Sharmila glared at her. She knew Alina didn't want to be there right now and had had a fight with Emilio, but this was rude.

"Ah, young lady. That is a wonderful question. My family has been doing this for many years, and it will be my honor to answer it and show you the magic that is pashmina. Come here and let show you something," Mr. Shaikh signaled to one of the salesmen to bring over a brown shawl, which he took out of its plastic wrapper.

"Now there are two things I am going to tell you. One is a fact, and one is a marketing gimmick. If you can tell me which one is true, I will give you a *real* pashmina stole, which is very expensive, as a gift. Are you ready?"

"Oh, yes. Now *this* is fun, Ma." Always up for a challenge, Alina looked interested, and her tone was a lot friendlier.

Mr. Shaikh took the shawl and held it in one hand. In his other hand he held what looked like a wedding ring. He put one corner of the shawl through the ring, then kept pulling it. The large shawl did the impossible—it passed completely through the ring without a hitch.

"So, you saw that. Now, the two statements. First, it is said that pure pashmina is made from the fur from the throat of a special type of goat, the Changthangi. They use the throat fur because it doesn't get sun and makes for a softer, more delicate, but very sturdy shawl. The second statement is that only pure pashmina can be passed through a ring. Which one is the gimmick? Let me add that a pure pashmina shawl can run up to a thousand dollars. Antique shawls can run to several thousands."

The three of them began to discuss which could be marketing hype. George confessed he had never bought a pashmina shawl and had no idea.

Alina said, "All right, I think the goat. That's marketing. I mean, the *throat fur*? That's just weird, and it would take forever to get enough to make one shawl. So I'll go with the goat."

Mr. Shaikh smiled. "Actually, it is the ring. I don't know who came up with that. There are so many people who come and insist on this, so I do it for them. But I know that any good-quality shawl here that may be only half pashmina can pass through the ring."

The salesmen swung into action and began to show them different colors of shawls in many patterns and weaves. Mr. Shaikh continued his commentary about the value of the shawls and the care that needed to be taken with them.

Alina gave a little gasp and smiled slyly. "What if I want to customize the embroidery on a shawl?"

"Yes, it will take a few weeks, but we can make some minor changes if you like. It will depend on what you have in mind. Now, here is our gift to you, even though you lost the challenge. I am honored that you have humored me." And with that, Mr. Shaikh gave Alina a grey stole with gentle pink waves woven into the fabric.

"Thank you. This is awesome. Ma, I'd like that red one, but I may have some customizations I want to make." Alina picked up a deep red shawl with mango-shaped figures along the edges.

"Yes, yes. Come—you can talk to the weaver, who is in a room upstairs. I don't know how much can be changed, but let's ask him," Mr. Shaikh said. Before Sharmila could ask, Alina was gone.

"At least she's showing some interest. She had been so lukewarm about this whole thing. I really thought she would want to know about her father's home," Sharmila confessed to George.

He shook his head. "It's hard for her, I'm sure. But, as I told you before, Kashmir has a way of getting deep into your soul, and once it does, you never want to let go. Like some people you meet."

Sharmila blushed and turned away to finish paying and Alina returned. "They will make my additions. Ma, thank you so much for this." She hugged her mother.

Sharmila smiled. Again, something good was coming of this trip. "Where to now, George? Are we going to see the resorts?"

"Actually, George, I am sooooo hungry. Is there a place that's *not* going to be part of the wedding that we can go to? Just this once?" An exasperated tone accompanied Alina's request.

"Yes, for sure," George said.

Sharmila said, "But wait, can you give me a few minutes? I want to see some of the other shawls. I think these would make good gifts for the wedding guests." She began to peruse the other shawls.

Much to Alina's relief, George signaled to Sharmila that they would wait for her outside and let her take her time finding just the right gifts.

As they stood on the deck of the boat, George decided to make an attempt to check in with Alina. "Is all okay with you, kiddo? None of my business, but I noticed you don't seem to be your normal cheery self."

"Yeah. Well, it is hard being away from Emilio and this stupid time difference doesn't help. He was complaining that he has to stay up too late to talk to me. Whatever." Alina looked hurt. She stared into the distance as the tourists began milling around. "Oh, and Ma's suggestion? She says to leave him *alone*. Let him study. Yeah, fine. But doesn't he miss me and want to talk to me?"

George pushed his hands into his jeans pocket and leaned back on the boat. "Want my opinion?"

"Well, no. But since you are taking me to lunch, I guess I should at least give you a shot."

"Well, thank you, young lady. I am honored," George said, chuckling. "This isn't really about the time difference, Alina. This is about you and him setting up clear communications and what you expect of each other. Instead of accusing and getting angry, is there a solution you can work out that will work for you both? Sometimes, I feel like we make life so complicated by just reacting. We need to learn to respond. So let me ask you, how can you respond?"

Before Alina could say anything, Sharmila joined them. "I'm ready. What's going on here? You two look like you are in a serious discussion."

"Ah, yes. I was telling her how little I know about Taylor Swift, and she is clearly seeing how uncool I am," George said, much to Alina's surprise.

Sharmila handed the bag she was holding to George. "Happy birthday, George. I wanted to get you a warm scarf from here. I hope it will keep you cozy in the crazy winter here."

"Oh, I had forgotten. Happiest of birthdays, George." Alina turned to him and gave him a tight hug.

"I am so honored you remembered. Thank you for this thoughtful gift. I will treasure it," he responded warmly.

He drove them back into town. They headed to Lal Chowk, filled with locals who were shopping, schoolgirls walking with their school bags, and most important, street vendors selling all kinds of foods.

"We're going *there*," George said. It was the street vendor who had the longest line. "He serves the best kebabs in town, and no, he doesn't do weddings."

The rest of the afternoon was spent eating and shopping. Sharmila found herself telling George more and more about her paintings and the exhibition sites that had hosted her work. They seemed to have crossed paths at the National Portrait Gallery in DC, but they had never actually met. Sharmila said that now, thanks to his encouragement, she was even thinking of holding an exhibition in Srinagar after the wedding. Oh, and how much she loved her new Instagram account.

"Wait—what? Ma … are you joining the twenty-first century? Social media? What did you call it? 'The devil that's destroying the youth of the day,' if I recall correctly. My mother on social media? The one thing you swore you would never, ever, ever do? Well, I'll be damned. Now how did this *miracle* occur?"

George gave her a sly look. "I convinced her that it was good for her. The world needs more of her art in it."

"Ohhh, I see. Okay. That's … nice." Alina at first seemed a bit annoyed that her mother would listen to George but not to her. She bit her cheek and pursed her lips, but then something clicked, and she laughed. "That *is* nice."

With that, they headed back to the hotel.

"Ma, can I talk to George a minute? Alone?" Alina asked. Sharmila nodded, surprised, and left them alone as she headed to the room.

Alina said, "So George, I thought about what you said. About responding and not reacting. I just miss Emilio and want to talk to him, and I know he misses me too. I feel bad that he has to stay up late. So I'm thinking, I can record video messages to send him and he can see them when he has time and respond with the same. What do you think?"

He gave her a hug. "This, kiddo, is just the beginning of your life together. Be honest with your needs. I promise, the right solution will emerge."

George left to go home and cook dinner. The hotel had found Alina a ticket for the evening's event, so when they got back to their room, she started to get ready.

Sharmila rested for an hour and then began to get ready for the evening ahead. She looked at herself in the mirror. Her small frame, draped in a white and red Chanderi-style shimmering silk saree embroidered with vibrant peacocks, seemed more alive than ever. She slipped on matching red and silver bangles. Then she fixed her makeup, gently adding deep black kajal kohl to her eyelids.

"What did you and George talk about, Alina? Is everything okay?" Sharmila asked, but instantly regretted it. "Sorry, you don't have to tell me. I didn't mean to pry."

"Actually, he gave me some great advice about dealing with Emilio. Anyway, I'm leaving now, Ma."

"Are you sure you wouldn't rather join us?"

Alina had joked with her earlier that day about bowing out of dinner with two boring Gen Xers.

"I'm flattered he invited me, but this is an easy pass for me, Ma. I know it's his birthday but I want to go hang out with people my own age. I've done almost everything you asked for, and yes, I have enjoyed it more than I thought I would. Now I'm gonna do my thing."

Sharmila had felt strangely relieved. As much as she wanted Alina there, she could not help but admit she wondered what it would be like to be alone with George in a more intimate setting, even if it was just a few hours. *She had been alone with men before. Why did this feel so different? Was it different?*

It was at that moment that reality set in.

Am I really doing this? Sharmila thought. She ran her hand over the saree, smoothing out wrinkles that didn't exist. She readjusted her diamond drop necklace and her solitaire earrings.

Maybe I'm overdressed? This isn't a date. It's just dinner with a friend. Or is it? Is it a date? No, no. I am not dating him. This is silly. But we are *friends, right? Was this too much makeup?*

She began to remove her bangles. Then put them back on.

This is silly. It's just dinner. We're just having dinner. It's fine.

The phone in her room rang. It was the front desk letting her know that the taxi she had requested was ready. "Yes, thank you, I will be right down."

The ride to George's houseboat took only about fifteen minutes, but to Sharmila it felt like a lifetime. She checked her phone every minute to see if perhaps he had cancelled, or if Alina had changed her mind and was going to join them.

This is silly, she chided herself. *It's just a dinner. Everything is fine. I'm a grown adult. He's an adult. There's nothing to be nervous about.*

The taxi dropped her off at the boat, and now as she stood face to face with George, she felt an inexplicable connection with the man standing before her. His warm smile and eyes reflecting the shimmering water drew her in. Even the air between them felt different. Electric. As Sharmila stepped onto the houseboat, she hoped that the rhythmic swaying of the boat would calm her nervousness.

"Happy birthday, again. I feel guilty making you cook. I would've offered, but I can't cook, and lucky you, they have no kitchen at the hotel that I could use." Sharmila laughed nervously.

"You look gorgeous," George told her with a smile fit for a movie star. "Please come in. This isn't as fancy as Sukoon, but it's the second love of my life. The first one being, well, food."

Inside his houseboat, named Zuva, the atmosphere was peaceful and inviting. Colorful pillows with tilla embroidery were strewn about casually. There was a large couch on one side. Embroidered fabrics in frames hung all around the small boat.

"What does Zuva mean?" Sharmila asked.

"Oh, it's Kashmiri for *soul mate*, or more aptly, I guess it's a term of love for the person who is your soul or life."

"That's beautiful. Here, this is for you," Sharmila nervously handed him a small bouquet of brightly colored roses wrapped around an old branch.

"Ah, I see you've been in touch with our flower lady, Zarina. Thank you, and I do think this is a first. I don't remember the last time a woman, or I guess anyone, brought me flowers. And thank you again for the scarf. It *is* warm, and I know I will get a lot of use out of it."

Did she detect a bit of pink in his cheeks? Was he blushing?

Sharmila thought he seemed nervous too, but decided she was clearly overthinking the situation. She stared at the framed art on the wall while she focused her thoughts. It was just a dinner between two adults. That was all. *Why would he be nervous?*

"Ah, all these that you're looking at? This is what Daneen's true love was. Tilla work. I keep a few of her pieces here."

"This is her here, right? She's so lovely. These are delightful pictures, George." Sharmila picked up a silver frame with a photograph of Daneen and George in front of the National Press Club in Washington.

"Ah, yes. She had an exhibition of her work there that day. It was pretty exciting. Seems like a lifetime ago."

"Something smells really good," Sharmila said, changing the

topic as she noticed the sadness in his eyes.

"Tonight I'm cooking you a trout curry. I caught this fish today," he boasted, but somehow it didn't sound quite like a boast. From what she already knew of him, he wasn't one to boast about any of his accomplishments. She waited for the punchline.

"Well, actually the fish lady just came by on her shikara and sold it to me, but that doesn't sound as good, does it?" He laughed at his own joke.

It was the first time she had seen him laugh like that. He seemed so comfortable in his quiet home here. His guard was down. His steps firmer. He was humming as he moved to the small cooker that served as the kitchen on the boat.

"I smell saffron and cardamom and ... something else?" she said, walking up to him at the stove.

"Yes, keep trying to guess what the third smell is," he said as his hands moved, skillfully blending the aromatic ingredients into a paste that he then added to a pot already on the stove. The mixture in the pot sizzled, and George continued to work. She watched him expertly fillet the trout before adding it to the pot. Watching him cook with such passion and care stirred something deep within Sharmila, awakening feelings she had suppressed for so long. *His hands move so gracefully.*

She found a quiet corner from where she could observe him without being in the way. In her heart, she worried he could sense her longing. *That's impossible. He isn't a mind reader.*

She continued looking around the houseboat. A few lines from Rumi's poetry echoed in her mind:

Let yourself be silently drawn

By the strange pull of what you really love
It will not lead you astray

These words resonated deeply with her as she watched George, feeling so drawn to him. She looked away, embarrassed. And yet the *what if?* rang in her head.

She shook her head to clear it and looked outside. The usually calm lake wasn't so calm this evening. A storm was brewing and there were unseemly ripples all over. *They are mirroring my heart,* Sharmila thought.

She turned around to look at him again. Sharmila noticed the delicacy with which he handled each ingredient, the passion in his eyes as he went about cooking. Her fears began to dissolve, and she felt an urge to bridge the gap between them, to break free from the barriers she'd built around her heart. *I want to hug him and place my head on his shoulder. Just once.*

As he stirred the pot, he talked about the rice he was making. "You know, I always thought fish curry and rice complete each other. Like soul mates. But now I don't think that's it. I think they awaken something in each other that's dormant without the other."

Sharmila stood still. He wasn't talking about the food. Or was he? She couldn't tell anymore.

"Are you ready to eat?" George said as he tasted the curry. "It's ready."

They sat down at the small dinner table and began to eat. George began to tell her colorful tales of his experiences in Srinagar. Sharmila couldn't help but laugh at his gentle, self-deprecating manner.

"I get the feeling that Alina is finally warming up to getting married here?" he asked Sharmila as they finished the meal.

"Yes, and I am so grateful. And, well, there is one other thing that I haven't told her yet and I don't know how she will react ..."

George began to clear the table and added casually, "Is this something to do with the police inspector you were speaking with earlier?"

"Oh, how did you know? Did you see him at the hotel? You saw?" She took a deep breath. "I'm trying to find Vikram's family. They used to live in Lal Mandi, but now I don't know where they are. He was helping, but he couldn't find any leads. They moved a while ago and I don't know. I thought maybe I could meet them. I don't actually know what I thought would happen. Maybe it just isn't meant to be." Sharmila couldn't sit anymore, so she got up to help clear the table and the two found themselves close to each other at the small kitchen sink.

"Maybe I can help. Could you share the details with me and Wajid? Only if you're comfortable doing that, of course."

Sharmila nodded. "I have an old address and their names. I'll text them to you. Please don't mention it to Alina yet. I don't want her to be disappointed if I can't find them."

"They were Kashmiri Pandits, right? This would have been in the early to mid-nineties? That was the time the unrest started in Kashmir—many Kashmiri Pandits left Srinagar and settled in Jammu. Some even moved to the outside areas of Pahalgam. Not all voluntarily," George added as he tried to recall that time. It was the same time he and Daneen got married. They had had a civil marriage, as his religion was different.

"Yes, it was. I only know that his name was Vikram Pandit and that his family was in Lal Mandi. I tried to reach out to the person who had hired him for his painting studio, but everything was so hard back then, and I lost touch with them."

"Painting studio?"

"Yes, that's how I met him. He was a painting instructor who had come into town, and he inspired me to start painting seriously. Then, well, things went terribly wrong when he returned here." Sharmila's voice began to quiver as the dark memories came back.

"Would you like to dance?" George changed the topic in an instant, moving away from the sink and putting on some music. Now he was standing in front of her.

"Wait. What?"

He held out his hand.

"It is my birthday, so I thought a dance would be fun. Let's change the mood, shall we? I'll help you find his family. Don't worry. Now, let's dance."

Her carefully composed façade was failing her now. She reached out and took his hand. Once again, it was warm in hers. Their eyes met and lingered for a moment. *What is happening here?* Sharmila wondered. *I need to stop this. I am here for Alina's wedding. I am too old for this.*

The houseboat shook as the storm outside began to build.

He tenderly pulled her closer to him as the music took over and they began to sway to the rhythm of the guitar playing.

Her heart skipped a beat, torn between the desire to indulge in the moment and the fear of betraying her desire to stay content being alone for the rest of her life.

His presence had a calming effect. She could detect a blend

of his cologne with the faint aroma of cardamom and saffron on his breath, which was oddly reassuring. There was a warmth that provided a sense of security, like being at home.

As they swayed to the rhythm, an invisible energy enveloped them. His hand gently rested on her waist, pulling her closer, and once more she felt a desire she hadn't experienced in years. The boat rocked them. It was as though they didn't even need to move. Nature was lending a helping hand.

With every step they took, a subtle chemistry blossomed between them, drawing them together in a dance of longing. The outside world dissolved into insignificance, and for a brief instant, they found themselves alone, wrapped in a wordless connection.

As the song reached its melancholic crescendo, Sharmila felt a pang of fear—or was it guilt? She knew that she was on the precipice of something significant, and yet the idea of being intimate with a man frightened her. The past had left its scars, and she couldn't bear the thought of being hurt again.

With a sudden resolve, she pulled away from his embrace, her eyes a mix of sadness and regret.

"I'm sorry," she whispered, her voice barely audible above the music. "I can't do this. Not now."

He looked at her, a touch of disappointment flickering in his eyes, but he understood. Love, after all, could not be forced. He nodded, managing a faint smile, trying to hide his own vulnerability.

In that moment, they both knew that something had shifted between them. George closed his eyes, and the ill-fated words of the fortune teller filled his head, reminding him that there was to be no love in his future.

Sharmila turned towards the doorway, trying to keep her composure. Tears welled up in her eyes, emotions overwhelmed her heart. Then she turned back to look at him.

"Roses, right?"

"What roses?" he asked, perplexed.

"That smell, the one that I couldn't tell earlier. It's roses, right?"

"Oh my, yes, I almost forgot. I made you dessert. Phirni—pudding with rosewater and rose petals. Yes, that's the smell. Please stay. We can eat that together … as friends, yes? It is my birthday so don't make me eat dessert alone." He looked hopeful but was clearly so hesitant.

Sharmila came back towards him.

"Yes, we can. I can't leave a meal incomplete."

They ate in silence. The air was lighter. The ripples in the lake had stopped. The storm had passed.

Chapter 10

"It has been almost a week now and I finally feel human again." Alina's voice was filled with relief as she talked to Emilio on a video call. "I didn't think it was going to be so long."

A week earlier, she had come back to the hotel room after the Taylor Swift tribute show and told Sharmila that something was bothering her stomach. That something turned out to be a food allergy. Alina was allergic to mushrooms and in the midst of a fun evening didn't realize that the rice she was eating had tiny bits of sautéed mushrooms. Since then, she had been stuck in the room, throwing up and dealing with stomach cramps.

"I am glad you are better, and I am happy to see you smiling. Of course, with your mom there, I have to say that I wasn't too worried." Emilio smiled into the camera.

It was late in the day in Srinagar but early morning for Emilio, who was back in Washington. He had insisted on talking to her live now that she was feeling better. Alina turned the camera to show him the stunning view through the hotel window. Lined up on the windowsill were bottles of fresh water, a fruit bowl filled with Kashmiri apples, and a large vase of white and pink roses.

"I am actually looking forward to coming there and seeing you and those mountains in person."

Alina told him how not only her mother had cared for her, but George, too.

"He was here every day—well, you know that since we sent you videos of us. But seriously, he was here with the doctor, then with the medicines, and then making sure I wasn't bored. Oh, and those roses I showed you in the window? That's from him. He's been bringing me fresh roses every day—this room is filled with flowers."

"Looks like I may have some competition there," Emilio said.

"Very funny. I don't think I have played so many card games since I was a kid, and I have to say, sick or not sick, I beat him and Ma at Scrabble four times. He is a sweetheart," Alina said. In fact, during the week, she had confided in her mom that it was hard to believe George didn't have children as he came across as a warm father figure, very patient and caring.

"As you know, I am not a bundle of joy to be around when I am sick, Emilio. Yet he kept his patience with me even though he didn't need to be here."

Emilio listened for a few minutes as Alina went on and on about George and her stomach and all the issues. "You know, Alina, my nonna has always told me that the best relationships are not necessarily the ones that are due to blood relations. They are the ones where people care for you and love you because of who you are and who they are." He went on to ask how Sharmila's relationship was with George.

"Ma? She likes him a lot. She seems happy here, Emilio. I see her painting with abandon here. I mean, when was the last time you saw Ma laughing like a little kid? One thing I noticed, I guess, now that you're asking. I see Ma asking him endless questions. I have never seen that side of her before. She is so curious, like a child. Anyway, now they've gone on a walk."

She added that she had to push them out of the room so she could talk to him privately as they didn't want to leave her alone.

"Well, then, we should make use of this privacy, shouldn't we," he said and leaned into the camera to give her a kiss.

For the next few minutes, Alina and Emilio were as intimate as modern technology would allow. "I miss you and I am coming home soon," Alina said.

"I can't wait to see you. Alina, do you think your mom actually likes George? As in, you know, a possible relationship, or is it just a friendship?"

"Hmm … I have been wondering. Ma has always been, you know, alone. I don't know," Alina said, but his words made her think.

About an hour or so after Alina hung up the phone, Sharmila and George entered the room, holding bags filled with fresh fruit and a large tub of soup. Alina knew that tub well. Wajid had been sending homemade broth to make sure she was getting her nutrients, as he was worried that the hotel food wasn't going to cut it.

"Joy, joy, more soup," Alina said wryly.

"Well, young lady, you are wrong. This time, it isn't. Wajid was insisting on more soup, but since you are feeling a lot better, this time it is rice with chicken from my kitchen. So please, prepare to be impressed," George said.

He opened the container and the smell of cinnamon and fried

onions filled the room. Alina didn't need any other invitation and ate the rice he gave her. With every bite, she complimented his cooking and thanked the Lord for real food that wasn't soup.

Sharmila sat across from her and ate too but looked very somber.

"What is the matter, Ma? You don't like George's cooking?" Alina asked.

Before Sharmila could answer, George jumped in. "I think she is back on that island you always joke about—the island of worry. Is that what you call it?"

Sharmila shook her head at them. "You both think you are so cool. Well, I *am* worried. We are to head back soon, and we are nowhere near the wedding planning being completed here. I don't know how we will do it from there," she said softly.

The three continued to eat in silence. Then Alina spoke up.

"Ma, why don't we extend the trip for another three weeks? I don't mind staying a bit longer. Emilio is busy with his exams now and when we get back, he will be off for Thanksgiving. What do you think? I really think I want to stay here and learn more. I am glad you suggested this, Ma. I am so glad."

Within minutes, the dates were shifted, and the trip was officially extended. A very relieved Sharmila sat back on the hotel room couch and sighed. "Now we can plan. I am so glad you agreed to this. But even more glad that you are feeling better."

Alina watched Sharmila and George clean up the dinner plates as they talked and joked about taking care of her. Their movements were in sync, as though they had been together a long time. She cleared and handed him the trash. He moved the dirty glasses and placed them outside the door. She called housekeeping to clean up, and he sat down and made a list of the things that they were going to do the next few weeks. They laughed more than they talked.

"Sharmila, I'm going to leave now. I'll be busy with Wajid for the next day or so on that mission we discussed. But I'll be back shortly and then, Ms. Alina, we can continue our tour and get you ready for a fabulous Kashmiri-style wedding."

When he left, Sharmila went to the bathroom to get ready for the night.

Alina wondered what the mission was. More importantly, she thought about the way Sharmila reacted when Alina suggested they push the trip out for a few more weeks.

The way Sharmila's eyes had lit up told Alina a lot more than Sharmila probably wanted to share.

Chapter 11

"Sharmila, you aren't going to believe this." George's voice was filled with excitement. "I didn't think our mission to find Vikram's family was going to be easy."

He had been gone a few days, texting her updates. Alina felt better, so she and Sharmila used the time to revisit Raahat and talk more to Zarina about the flowers. And much to Alina's delight, to spend some more time visiting some of the smaller tea shops and just soak up the atmosphere before the brisk winds of winter arrived.

"About Vikram? Shh … Alina is here," Sharmila placed a finger on her lips.

George was standing at the door of Sharmila's hotel room. Dressed in what Alina called his "old man's uniform"—a pair of blue jeans and a white cashmere sweater—he looked relaxed and content.

After their awkward night on his houseboat, Sharmila had been worried that would make seeing him again very difficult. But then he showed up and helped with Alina's illness with his easygoing and warm manner. All her worry was replaced with a longing yet again. Their walks during that time were filled with stories about his younger days and hers. They talked about schoolmates and parents, about school grades and college graduations. Sharmila had always felt "less than" since she hadn't gone to college, but he made her realize that a schoolbook education wasn't all that mattered. Sometimes they talked a lot on the walks, sometimes they just walked with no words. She told him about the draft poetry book that she had been working on for over a decade but hadn't had the courage to publish as she didn't have a degree.

"I'm an art professor and I can't paint anything," he said. "We all have our talents, and you have so many. I would love to hear the poetry."

Their last few walks were filled with her reciting her poetry about love, longing, and finding peace. He asked many questions, but more than anything encouraged and praised her hidden talent. "You have the ability to paint with a brush *and* with words. Just keep doing what makes your heart sing," he told her.

Now, he was here, at her door with a big smile on his face and holding flowers for Alina.

"Alina, come here, please. George is here," Sharmila called. Alina was on the bed, talking to Emilio on a video call.

During the past week, George and Emilio had talked frequently on video calls and had taken an instant liking to each other.

"Hopefully we can convince your bride-to-be to have her wedding in our valley. She's a hard lady to convince."

"I understand she is softening her stance now and is going to stay a bit longer?" Emilio asked.

After hanging up the call, Alina turned towards the others. "So, George, I was telling Emilio that I'm going to be doing something different today. I met a bunch of hikers last night in the hotel lobby. They're heading out for a trek and I think I may join them. Sounds like fun." Alina shrugged and pulled out her phone as it buzzed nonstop.

"Are you sure you're feeling up to it, Alina? Your stomach is okay?" Sharmila asked.

"*Ma*, that was over a week ago. Yes, I'm fine. And I've done enough shopping and eating. I just need to do something different. Okay?" She disappeared into the bathroom.

Sharmila sighed but knew Alina well enough to know when she needed a break. George stepped close and lowered his voice.

"She's fine now. Let her go. I think I found a link to Vikram's family. We can check that out today, and then tomorrow, if all goes well, we can take Alina there."

Alina returned and saw that her mother's face had a peculiar, almost bewildered expression. "Ma, are you okay? What happened? Are you upset that I'm not joining you? You can do one more wedding thing without me, right? George, what's on the agenda today?"

Before George could take a breath to answer, Sharmila was firing questions at Alina about not having trekking gear, not having the right clothes, and she began to worry out loud.

George said, "Sharmila, we have to visit a few resorts today—you and I can do that. Let her go on her adventure. Kashmir does have shops where she can buy what she needs. I can take you to the other valley that I want to show you."

Sharmila ordered some tea from room service. Soon, Alina

was dressed and ready. As she opened the door to leave, there was a waiter outside who brought in the tea service. He set it up on the main table, then left.

"Do you really think you found something? Where?" Sharmila poured tea into cups. She tried to steady her nervous hands and hoped George didn't see her hands shaking. She couldn't tell if she was nervous being so close to him and alone again in a room or because he had found a contact for Vikram's family—or both.

"You mentioned that they were in Lal Mandi, right? For the last few days, Wajid and I have been calling and meeting many people who were here in the early nineties. Finally, I found an old friend who remembered something. You recall my telling you, many Pandits left that area and moved to Jammu? My friend, who works for the city, found a record of a Pandit family that had two sons, that they lost one of the sons, a painter, and then moved to Aru Valley. The ages and the timing seemed about right. I actually confirmed all this with Wajid's father-in-law, who is a judge in the courts here."

Sharmila sipped her tea, taking in the information. "I've tried to find them on and off for years now. Every lead was a dead end. How can you be sure it's them?"

George pulled out his phone and showed her a picture. He had taken a photo of the entry in the record book. It clearly stated that the people at the Lal Mandi address she had provided had moved to Aru Valley under the auspices of the local government after their son was possibly gunned down and reported missing in crossfire on the Gawkadal Bridge.

"That's a lot of coincidences, I know. But I think we can drive up there and see what happens," George said.

Sharmila looked at the image in disbelief. She stood up. "Yes, let's go. I'm ready."

George checked his phone again for weather conditions and looked at her. "Sorry, but you need to change. Aru Valley will be colder than here, and you're going to need sturdy walking shoes. *And* we can ride horses part of the way. You can ride, I hope."

A few minutes later, dressed in jeans and her warm black sweater, Sharmila joined him in the Jeep. He was on the phone, talking a mile a minute with someone trying to figure out the best way to drive to the Aru Valley. Sharmila gathered it must have been Wajid on the other end.

"It will take a good three hours to get there. I think we can make it there by lunch time," George said as he began the drive. At first, the two of them were quiet as the Jeep made its way through the crowded streets of Srinagar. Sharmila was answering texts from Alina, who was now on her way to the trek and very excited to be doing something not wedding-related.

Once they were out of the noisy city, Sharmila broke the silence.

"I have to admit, I am more than a bit nervous about this. I don't even know if they know that I or Alina exist. I just don't know how they will react to us. What if they hate us? Maybe this isn't a good idea."

"Yes, I can imagine you are nervous. But you know, I have lived here on and off for half my life, and most Kashmiris are gentle and soft-spoken. Even when they get upset, it sounds like they're giving you a blessing. Anyhow, I am sure they will want to learn more about how you both met and of course, how he taught you to paint."

Sharmila smiled despite her nerves.

"You know, George, I was so young then, I had never met anyone like him. He was intense and in love with his craft. His paintings were vivid and captured the most visceral of emotions. I liked his landscapes, but when he painted a face, it took my breath away. That is what I remember mostly. We were together for less than a year and a half. Young, happy, carefree, and yes, mostly covered in paint," Sharmila said.

George nodded. "Oh, to be young and in love. I remember those days well. Goes by fast, doesn't it?"

"It does indeed. My family was very conservative and I knew they wouldn't accept Vikram." Sharmila went quiet for a few moments as though debating whether she should share anything else about her family. It had been ingrained in her never to speak about them in public.

The trees on the side of the roads were starting to shed their golden leaves. Winter wasn't too far away, but the sun was warm so the open Jeep convertible was still good to travel in.

"Are you okay? I didn't mean to pry," George said, then asked her to open the thermos of hot tea.

"It will take something a lot stronger than hot tea to get me to talk much about them," she said as she sipped the tea.

Sharmila had been born into a deeply conservative family with roots in the Rajasthani royal bloodline. Both her parents were strict and followed the rules of the royalty even to their detriment. While her father did want her to go to college, her mother was determined to get her married at a young age. Sharmila had revolted. She wanted to study, but there was no way it was going to happen. Then she met Vikram. She hesitatingly told George about how her parents looked down on Vikram in every way. Vikram's family was from a poor background and her father would not even deign to talk to him.

George stopped the Jeep and the two of them got down and tried a roadside snack, an all-India favorite, spiced noodles. The unusual touch, George told Sharmila, was that this vendor added scrambled eggs to the noodles—a taste that had to be tried to be believed.

He stretched his legs and sat down on the side of the road for a few minutes.

"I'm sorry about the difficulties. It is hard with conservative families. My own never accepted Daneen, so I just moved away from them. Such hatred towards her because of her religion. Yours was for money reasons. I guess to each his own."

Sharmila nodded.

George pulled the top over the Jeep since it looked like it was going to start raining, and the weather had already started to cool down as they approached Pahalgam.

They got back in the Jeep and continued on their journey.

"And your pregnancy? That was difficult for them, right?" George picked up the conversation again.

"They were so angry. I was already the black sheep and then, you know, pregnancy out of wedlock," Sharmila said, adding that Vikram wanted to marry her as soon as possible. He felt sure his family would be very accepting if he told them in person and so he'd gone back to Kashmir to inform them. "I remember pleading with him not to leave, but he had a point. This wasn't the type of news he wanted to break to them over a long-distance call. His father was ill, and his mother was not quite herself. He thought a call like that would really upset them. The plan was for him to bring them back to Jaipur, but that never happened."

"How did you find out what happened when he came back here? I remember the communications infrastructure back then was terrible," George asked and, seeing the pain on her face, instantly regretted the question. "I'm so sorry."

She explained that someone had called the painting studio to inform them that Vikram had been involved in some attack. But there was no other information to be found. She said she regretted not getting any information from him before he left. She had never imagined that she would never see him again.

They had already entered the picturesque area of Pahalgam. The narrow roads into the valley had been filled with green fields, but it seemed like the two of them were more involved in each other and their stories than in looking at scenery.

For Sharmila, the memories flooded in. Her father was even more furious after the phone call. He ordered her to his study, from which he ruled his family as though it were his kingdom. "You have ruined the family name, and there is no forgiveness for you now. I will not have an unwed mother in this house. I have arranged for you to go to America, to Washington, and to stay in our house there. You will be provided a sufficient amount of money from your trust fund. Now leave." She never saw her mother or father again.

"They died without even seeing Alina once. I tried to contact them, but you know, according to him his word was law. My sister, I'm trying to see if she will attend this wedding, but—"

Before Sharmila could finish, George had stopped the Jeep in a parking lot near the main tourist center in Aru Valley.

"Come on. We have to get on the horses here to go up from this point. There is another paved road up on the other side, but I think you will enjoy the horse ride as you will get to see the heart of this Aru this way."

As the horse ride began, Sharmila gasped as she looked around. Lush green meadows were dotted with a sprinkling of wildflowers. The snow-capped peaks of the mountains just in front of them stood majestically against the bright blue sky. The young man who had provided them with horses pointed out the clear water of the Lidder River.

"Can we stop a minute?" Sharmila said. "George, can we stop, please?"

"What is it?" George said, and asked the young man who was leading their horses to stop.

"George, I don't know if I can do this. What if they hate me? What if they aren't the right people? I'm getting anxious. I've dreamt of this moment half my life, but now I'm not sure I want to go through with it."

"Sharmila, I don't know if I have the right people, but I can assure you, if they are, they will love you. Who can not love you? I mean, you *and* Alina," George said, flustered.

The ride up to the main village continued. Sharmila saw kids from the local Gujjar tribe cutting grass, presumably gathering it to feed their livestock in the coming winter. The few wooden houses in front of them were small, with blue tarps on the roofs in preparation for the oncoming snowstorms.

The young man who had rented them the horses said something to George in Kashmiri. George handed him some money and turned to Sharmila.

"We'll walk from here on in." George offered Sharmila his hand without saying anything else. She didn't hesitate and, with a gentle smile, placed her hand in his. As their fingers intertwined, their unspoken connection comforted her and calmed her nerves. But as soon as he pointed to the house, she pulled her hand away.

"Thank you for doing this with me, George. I appreciate you," she whispered.

He nodded. "Here, this is it."

In front of them was a small, weathered cottage, nestled in the bosom of Aru Valley's serenity. The stone and log walls of the cottage were bathed in hues of an earthy brown. The sides of the cottage were covered in moss and greens that seemed to begin at the top of the cottage and merge seamlessly into the ground with the valley's lush foliage.

Sharmila's eye caught the patchwork of shingles on the roof that had clearly seen many years of snow, frost, and thaw. There were even a few wildflowers that appeared to emerge from the thatch as though defying the oncoming winter. She noticed the small but luscious garden that encircled the cottage. Dainty, soft white flowers mingled with hardy herbs everywhere in the garden. A tiny brook ran by the side of the cottage. A few feet away from the brook, a man was chopping firewood.

"Hello, is this the home of Vikram Pandit?" George asked in Kashmiri.

The man looked up. He dropped his ax and the wood in surprise. He was about to say something when a much older woman came out of the house and joined him.

Sharmila said, "I think we *are* at the right place. That man, he looks so much like Vikram. I wonder if that is—" She stopped as the man approached her and George.

"I am Suraj Pandit, and this is my mother. Who are you? Why are you asking about Vikram?"

The elderly lady walked up to Sharmila. She raised her hand to touch Sharmila's face, then looked at her son, Suraj. She turned back to Sharmila and looked at her face again as if trying to remember something.

"My name is Sharmila. We are looking for Vikram," Sharmila said, as the woman kept looking at her. Then the woman nodded at Suraj. She asked them to wait and went back into the house.

"Vikram was my older brother," Suraj said. "He has been gone for a while. I don't recognize your name, but you do look so familiar."

His mother came back out. In her hands was a painting.

"Oh my God. That is me in that painting. Oh my God. This is it, you *are* Vikram's family." Sharmila's words came out fast and frantic.

The painting featured a young, pregnant Sharmila, dressed in a deep blue outfit, her hands over her belly, smiling at the artist. The painting had Vikram's unique signature.

Vikram's mother pointed to the painting, asking if that was indeed her. Sharmila took the old lady's hand and began to speak softly. "Yes, that is me. Vikram and I were … but …"

Sharmila couldn't contain the surge of the emotions she had buried for so many years. They now unfurled in her heart, and tears welled up in her eyes, blurring the beauty of the valley, the painting, and everything else before her.

Vikram's mother, standing beside a blossoming wildflower bush, clutched the painting, which was the last thing that she had of Vikram's in her possession. It was the only thing that the policemen had given her. Tears welled up in her eyes, and a quiver touched her lips as she tried to hold back her own emotions.

Suraj, who had been quietly watching, was not immune to the overwhelming tide of feelings that enveloped them all. Sadness crept into his eyes, and he wiped an errant tear. His memories of Vikram had faded, and he barely remembered anything except that Vikram painted, and according to his mother, could survive on a diet of butter and more butter.

George stood silently aside. He couldn't help but admire the painting. The stunning masterpiece bore the marks of time—its vibrant colors had faded, and delicate brushwork was obscured by the touch of years. Despite its weathered appearance, he could see the bittersweet emotions the painting stirred were raw and powerful.

They all stood together in the garden, under the open sky, and wept. It was only for a few minutes, but it seemed longer. The fragrance of the wildflowers mingled with the scent of nostalgia as tears became the language of the moment. It was a moment of emotion—a tribute, it seemed, to Vikram's enduring presence in their memories.

It was Sharmila who spoke first. "Was it you who called our painting studio in Jaipur, Suraj? I recall it was a man who called, but I didn't know who it was."

"No, it was my uncle who called the studio. He spoke to a man there to tell them that Vikram had gone missing, and was presumed dead like all the others on the bridge that day. His best friend, Afzal, died. We lost so many from our neighborhood."

Vikram's mother took Sharmila's hands and kissed them. She pointed to the painting again, specifically to Sharmila's pregnant belly.

Sharmila gently pulled a hand away to take out her phone. "Here. This is a picture of your granddaughter, Alina. She is getting married here in Srinagar next spring. I would like you to meet her. Would you like that? I'm sorry, I am struggling with words. We had given up hope of finding you." She stumbled through her words, overwhelmed with emotions. "George, he made it possible. He found the records."

Cheers and hugs answered her. Sharmila turned to George and mouthed *Thank you.* He simply smiled as Vikram's mother took Sharmila inside the house. He sat outside on a small chair as Suraj served him some kahwa.

George called Wajid. "We're here and she seems very happy. Emotional, of course. I just … this is hard for me. I don't know why."

He didn't say that he was worried about losing her to this family. It seemed to be his superpower—losing people he loved.

Chapter 12

The inside of the cottage was warm and framed in aged wood. The windows peered at the valley around. The glow of the small metal fireplace danced on the worn wooden floors. The cottage's interior was a haven of comfort and simplicity. A low wooden table, polished by years of use, commanded the center of the room. Handwoven rugs adorned the floor, their intricate patterns echoing the tapestry of the valley itself. Sharmila noticed the kitchen was filled with an assortment of pans and pots and lined with clear jars filled with homemade pickles. Small shelves held jars filled with fragrant spices.

Sharmila felt instantly at home. The energy bore witness to the loving lives of those who called this place home. She sat down on the rug. Her phone buzzed—Alina had sent some pictures. Sharmila was surprised that her phone still had service in this remote area. But for the moment, she just ignored the incoming texts.

Vikram's mother prepared more kahwa and offered it to Sharmila. She sat down on the rug next to Sharmila and held her hand and kissed it again. Slowly, Sharmila began to tell her what had happened. She went through the memories slowly, carefully, not wanting to upset the older woman. She told her that they wanted to marry, that Vikram was coming home for her permission and that, of course, she had been pregnant.

"Your parents? Your parents are lucky to have you. I can see why he fell in love with you," Vikram's mother said in Hindi. "I feel sad that I lost my son, and I couldn't take care of my daughter-in-law during her time of need and have never taken care of my grandchild. I have failed Vikram in so many ways. But your parents, they are lucky. They must have taken care of you." When Sharmila explained what had happened with her, Vikram's mother appeared shaken. "This is the problem with us humans. We do not have gratitude for what God gives us. We want everything to be our way. But that is not God's way."

She decided it was time to feed them. She told Sharmila to call the gentlemen inside. Within minutes, she had heated up rice and lentils and prepared some chicken kebabs laced with cinnamon and cloves.

Sharmila and George sat with the family on the rug. Vikram's mother insisted on feeding them with her own hand, as though they were young children. She gave them each a single bite of rice with meat and then kissed their foreheads as tears rolled down her cheeks. "I cannot wait to meet my grandchild. I only wish Vikram was here. And Vikram's father. Poor man saw little joy in his life. He was very ill, died very young."

As the meal progressed, George gave Suraj details of how he found the family, adding that the note about the incident with his brother on that fateful bridge was what helped him make the connection.

"Yes, it was devastating for us. The police gave us the painting, but not much else."

The sun was getting ready to set. "You must head back now if you want to make it to Srinagar before too late," Suraj advised them. "The roads are menacing at night with all the traffic. You should head out to avoid getting stuck on the roads in the night. It isn't safe."

"I still cannot believe this is real," Sharmila said. "I wish Vikram was with us. But I know he must be happy that we are together." Sharmila added that she couldn't wait to introduce them to Alina. She considered video calling her daughter but then thought better of it. Vikram had been right—some news was better to give in person.

It was still almost an hour later before a radiant Sharmila and a relieved George were ready to head back to Srinagar. Vikram's mother called George over and kissed his forehead. She thanked him for making this meeting a reality, adding, "I did not know that there was anything left for me in my old age, but you have made an old woman very happy."

George bowed down to get her blessing, as was customary in that part of the region, and indicated to Sharmila to do the same. Vikram's mother was touched and hugged them both with promises to see them again very soon. And, of course, to meet Alina.

"George, Suraj said he will bring his mother to Srinagar in a day or so to meet Alina," Sharmila said. "I don't know how to thank you. You have become such an important part of my life in such a short time."

Suraj knew they needed fresh horses to trek to the parking spot where George had left his Jeep. He quickly arranged for a neighbor who owned horses, and often provided them for return journeys, to help George and Sharmila get back.

As they began their trip back to Srinagar, George noticed that Sharmila's whole demeanor had changed. She was now relaxed, but also excited about telling Alina. "This changes everything, George. We will finally have real family with us. I am so happy."

They drove back in the Jeep discussing the next steps—the catering and hotel and more.

"George, I meant to ask you earlier—how exactly did you find them? I know you asked around, but how did you know where to look?"

"Well, it's a rather long story," George said. "I have to take you back to 1993. At the old courthouse in the center of Srinagar." As he drove, he explained that it was the day of his civil marriage to Daneen. They had been inside the courthouse, getting ready to sign papers, and outside it was hell. Protests, grenades going off, gunfire—terrible.

"Our precious Kashmir was under attack. She and I had decided to get married. But it was so unsafe to live here back then. It broke our hearts to leave Kashmir." He stopped as he choked up.

He went on to explain that as soon as they had signed the register, a group of young people came in, talking about the Pandit families who were leaving. They were heading to Aru Valley or to the Jammu area. They were either escaping the violence voluntarily or being forced from their homes. This exile continued for the next few years. That sort of relocation would have been recorded at the courthouse, but most of the records had been destroyed when the courthouse was vandalized. However, there was an old judge who had saved some of the files.

As it happened, that judge was Wajid's father-in-law.

"I called Wajid and asked if he could ask his father-in-law. I think we just got lucky that someone in Vikram's family filled in the forms before they left. Most families, they just moved into camps, and no one heard from them again."

George didn't mention that there was something else he had discovered about the paperwork. Something possibly more sinister, or perhaps just missing. He was determined to find out which.

It was late when they returned to Srinagar. George stopped at a small roadside food stand on the edge of the city where they ate chicken biryani while planning out the next few days. Suraj had already messaged Sharmila some old photos of Vikram, and she couldn't wait to show them to Alina and tell her about her newly found family.

Just then her phone buzzed. It was a voice message from Alina. *Ma, how was your day? I am so tired from this trek, I am headed to bed. Talk to you in the morning, Ma. Please tell George I want to talk to him about other trekking spots here. It was simply amazing.*

Sharmila and George both smiled as they listened to the message. "Did I or did I not tell you that she will fall in love with the valley? You can feel free to say I told you so," George teased.

"Thank you, George. It isn't just her. It's because of you that I feel connected with life again too," Sharmila said. As George dropped her off at the hotel, she leaned in, kissed his cheek, and gave him a hug.

As she turned to go into the hotel, George whispered, "Yes, and because of you, I am connected to life, and love, again too."

Chapter 13

The next morning, Alina did not take the news about her father's family well. "You did what? How could you, Ma? I can't believe that you did it without me. And took George! Why didn't you *tell* me? How could you do this?" Alina's irritation turned quickly to frustration and ranting. "How could you keep this from me? Is *this* why you wanted to come to Kashmir? Did you even want to come for my wedding? How long have you been looking for him?"

"Alina, listen to me." Sharmila tried to interrupt but Alina kept going.

"I thought you told me that there was no way to find them. I remember when I was younger, you had been searching for them. And then, I remember you telling me that there was no trace of them. And now, now suddenly—"

Alina burst into tears. Sharmila took a deep breath. She hadn't expected this reaction. As a child, Alina was mostly fairly even-tempered, and rarely threw tantrums. But when something did rub her the wrong way, there was very little that could be done to calm her down.

"Why, Ma, *why*?"

Sharmila went over and hugged her daughter tightly, wiping her own tears.

"Alina, firstly, I am sorry. I was concerned that they would be angry with me. It's because of me that they lost their son. If that was the case, I didn't want you there to see that. I was just trying to protect you. I'm so sorry. I know you're not a child now. Please forgive me, Alina. I meant no harm. I did not know how they would react to me, to us."

A knock on the door startled them. Sharmila wiped her face and went to open it. It was George.

"What happened?" he asked when he saw her face. Then he saw Alina's tears and, with more urgency, asked, "What's wrong?"

"I'll tell you what's wrong, George." Alina was now standing with her arms crossed. "Why didn't you take me to see my grandmother? Why did you let my mom go without telling me? And now? What do you want, George?"

"Alina, that's no way to speak to him." Sharmila didn't want to lecture Alina, but this was downright disrespectful.

George's eyes were wide. He went to Alina and took her hands in his. "I'm sorry. I had no bad intent, Alina. Your mom and I were just trying to shield you in case things went south. Seriously, that's all."

Alina hadn't stopped crying. George wiped the remaining tears on her face. "You don't look so good with your eyes swollen like that. Tears are precious. Don't shed them for this. After all, this *is* good news."

"You didn't trust that I could handle this?" Alina all but screamed and pushed his hand away. "You should've told me."

Sharmila started to say something, but George motioned her

to stay quiet for a moment. He let Alina rant on for a few minutes. Finally, the tears subsided, and the girl collapsed on the couch.

It was then that George spoke again. "My sweet Alina. I am sorry. If you want me to leave, I will."

Sharmila sat by her daughter. "I am sorry. I guess I forget that you are an adult now and can handle tough situations. Not an excuse—I am just letting you know my intent wasn't to hurt you. I see, though, that I did, and I am so terribly sorry."

George brought Alina a glass of water and she reluctantly took it from him. He placed his hand on her head. "Alina, I have one thing to share. They want to meet you—they haven't stopped messaging me. They wanted to come here, but your grandmother changed her mind and asks that you go there instead. So today I'm here to take you to Aru Valley, if you want. I don't have to go with you, but I would really be honored to do so."

"This is wonderful. I knew they wanted to see her. I guess they're just as excited as I was to see them," Sharmila said. "They are kind, Alina. I can see where your father got his kindness from. Alina, we should go. What do you think? Don't let your anger affect your decision, please."

Alina finished drinking the water. And then nodded.

"I really want to meet them, plus you owe me for not taking me the first time, Ma." Calmer now, she got up and hugged her mom. "I am sorry I reacted so poorly. This is all too much to handle."

The three of them stood together in silence for a few moments, just holding space for all the emotions that swirled within them.

Alina broke away from the circle and went to the bathroom to wash up. She returned looking more settled.

"It feels unreal that there's someone from Dad's family who can tell me about him. I just accepted I'd never know more. This is good news—you're right, George."

Then she went to hug George, a gesture that caught both George and Sharmila by surprise. "Ma taught me that we only get really angry and upset at people we love and adore because we feel safe, deep in our hearts, that they will understand. Thank you for understanding. And Dr. George, while I do accept your apology, you still owe me big time for this."

George's pained look turned to relief and he immediately tuned into planning mode. He told them to pack some clothes in case they needed to stay there overnight. The weather was getting colder, and he thought they should be prepared.

"Oh, by the way, ladies, Wajid said you don't need to pay extra tour guide fees for the Aru Valley trips," George tried to joke. But Alina wasn't listening. She'd already pulled out a small bag and thrown in a few things. She hovered over her mom while she packed, then stood near the front door to indicate she was ready.

The three of them began the journey in George's Jeep. Now excited, Alina was adamant that her mother tell her everything she'd learned about the family. Every. Single. Thing. She wanted to know all the details before she met them.

When they finally arrived, Alina hesitated outside the cottage. She held George's hand on one side and her mother's on the other. She looked questioningly at her mom, then at George, who gave her hand a big squeeze.

George went to knock, but the door opened before his knuckles could make contact. Suraj greeted them with warm familiarity as they stepped inside to meet Vikram's mother.

In the corner of the room, the elderly woman sat on the edge of a bed. Her eyes filled with tears as soon as they fell upon Alina. She scrutinized the child from head to toe, as though trying to absorb every detail of her granddaughter's presence.

"Why is she crying, Ma? What's wrong?" Alina looked to her mother.

"Happy tears, child. These are the tears we want to shed. Happy tears."

With trembling hands, the grandmother motioned for Alina to approach. Her arms enveloped the young woman in a tight embrace, and she planted a series of soft kisses on Alina's forehead. With each kiss, she murmured words of blessing, each blessing carrying the weight of a lifetime of loss and yearning.

The old woman then reached beneath the thin mattress and retrieved an aged black-and-white photograph. Its corners were frayed, and it had faded with time. She held it up, her finger tracing the figure of her son, Alina's father, Vikram, frozen in a distant moment. Vikram was no older than twenty in the picture.

Turning her gaze between the photograph and Alina, she spoke in a voice filled with melancholy and love. Alina, unable to understand the words, turned to George, silently signaling him and requesting translation. George obliged, bridging the gap between generations and the cultures as he conveyed the grandmother's words.

In English and broken Hindi, Alina managed to explain to her grandmother that she was about to get married. She showed her grandmother pictures of herself and Emilio. The grandmother reached into a small bag she had by her side and pulled out an old red knitted scarf. She explained that it had belonged to Vikram and she wanted Alina to have it.

Finally, after about two hours of conversation, Alina took a deep breath, looked sweetly at her mother, and said, "Okay, Ma. *Now* this makes me *want* to have this wedding here. I would like to hold it in April, when the flowers are blooming, now that Grandma here has confirmed that spring is the best time to do it. And Ma, I'm sorry for earlier today."

Sharmila felt her nose tingle as tears of joy ran down her cheeks. Things could not be better. This was what she had always wanted. When it didn't seem things could get any sweeter, they did.

"We must get them a red pashmina shawl for Alina's posh puja, Suraj," the grandmother said.

Alina looked at George. "What is that?"

"This is for a special part of the wedding, Alina. It is one of the most beautiful rituals of Kashmiri Pandits. A shawl is draped over the couple as they sit together after the ceremony. The family then showers flower petals on the couple, marigolds and roses. It is a quite lovely, ritualistic way of blessing the couple for their new life together." Within minutes, Alina's grandmother was busy explaining to her what all the rituals were for a wedding, with George translating as best he could.

Suraj turned to Sharmila. "We insist you stay the night here. With your permission, I would like to take you all to Betaab Valley tomorrow. Alina, I will show you where Vikram painted. Would you like that?"

"Now that's an offer we can't refuse, right, Ma?" Alina was delighted. So was Sharmila. This was a perfect step forward for them as a family.

Dinner turned into a village gathering. All the neighbors came to meet Alina and Sharmila. Suraj created a small bonfire outside the house and everyone sat around it. At first, they wanted to know all about the two of them, having heard a little from the grandmother. But soon the fascination turned to the white American man who spoke good Hindi, decent Urdu, and, well, tried to speak Kashmiri, and also knew enough Bollywood tunes to want to join them in a fun little singing game called "Antakshari."

Alina leaned over to her mother. "What is Antakshari, Ma?" Sharmila explained that it was an Indian musical game where participants took turns singing songs, connecting each song's first letter or syllable to the last one of the previous song.

"It is a fun game, sort of like 'Name That Tune' in the US. I used to love it as a kid," she added.

With dinner done, everyone around the bonfire joined in and began to sing.

Alina didn't understand a word, and knew only a few songs from Shah Rukh Khan movies, but finally she felt a connection forming to the land of her father. The love was overwhelming, no matter the language.

They sang into the late hours of the night, feeding the bonfire and each other. Desserts kept coming from different neighbors, the songs getting louder, the clapping and the dancing more energetic. The whole village was rejoicing. The joy of one is the joy of all, Alina's grandmother explained to her.

Alina called Emilio at work to show him the scene and told him how meeting her grandmother had made her feel that a wedding here would be perfect.

"Yeah, sure, now you can talk to *my* mother, who's insisting on nuptials in Italy," he joked.

"Maybe we should just elope?" she teased with a laugh.

The melodious night ended. As Alina cuddled next to her mom that night, she whispered, "I can't wait to see where he painted, Ma. You're looking forward to it too, right?"

Sharmila patted Alina on the head. Yes, she was looking forward to it. But she was looking forward to spending another day with George too. That thought came so quickly, she didn't even have time to stop it. George had sat by her the entire evening, close. Sharmila wondered if anyone had noticed and then it occurred to her that perhaps she *wanted* Alina to see it.

To approve, perhaps, and even to accept.

Chapter 14

"We will first go to the gurudwara here and then head to Hagoon," Suraj declared bright and early in the morning.

Alina looked confused. "I thought you were taking us to Betaab Valley?"

Suraj smiled and explained that the original name for the valley was Hagoon, and that it got the name Betaab after an Indian movie was shot there. "Us locals prefer to call it by its original name. I go up there all the time. It is my place for solace and peace."

"Oh, I didn't know that. By the way, does 'Betaab' mean anything?" Alina asked.

"Eager," Suraj, George, and Sharmila all blurted out at the same time and started laughing.

Alina said goodbye to her grandmother, who sadly told her that she felt too tired to go with them for the whole day. The rest of them were ready in no time. Suraj packed a small tent for protection from the elements, and also a picnic consisting of aloo paranthas (potato-stuffed flatbreads), his mother's homemade mango pickle, and some fried lotus stems.

A famous gurudwara, a Sikh temple, was just a few

kilometers' driving distance from the house. As soon as they arrived, Sharmila gasped. "This place, I know this place. I've heard about it. Wait—"

"I thought this is your first time visiting Kashmir?" Suraj looked confused. Alina and George just smiled and nodded to each other. It was, as they expected, another painting Sharmila had made based on Vikram's description.

Sharmila was engrossed in her phone, scrolling through, looking for something. She found it. "Look—look at this painting I made years ago. I remember Vikram telling me about a place he used to visit, a yellowish building with what I thought was a pink awning and tall flowers growing in front of it. In fact, they are pink flowers, see there, and it's the flagpole that is yellow. I couldn't quite remember what he said it was."

Suraj said sweetly, "Gurudwara Chhevin Patshahi was one of his favorite places to offer prayers. He wasn't very religious, but if there was one place he believed in, it was this. Please come in. We will offer our prayers and then stay for the langar, the blessed meal held after prayers, before we head to the Hagoon Valley."

All of them entered the serene yellow room of the gurudwara. The priest welcomed them and invited them to sit for a while and absorb the blessings of the divine temple.

They all covered their heads with the colorful scarves provided by the temple staff, then stepped into the main room.

Alina, George, and Suraj sat together at the back of the room as Sharmila went up to the manji sahib, a raised platform that held the Sikh holy book. It was draped in shining pink silk. She bowed and touched her forehead to the floor, offering prayers of gratitude for her family, all the blessings that had been showered on her, and—she admitted it there—for George. She was grateful for him, his presence, his gentleness—and what she could only feel in her heart, the deep connection that she felt coming from him. Then she went back and sat next to the group.

"I want to go outside and check out the gardens," Alina whispered, and Suraj got up as well. The two went up to the manji sahib, prayed, and left.

"Do you want to go up and offer prayers, George?" Sharmila asked. He seemed usually quiet.

"Our time together is coming to an end, isn't it? You'll be leaving in a few weeks," he said softly, then went to pray.

Before Sharmila could think about what he said, her phone buzzed. Alina texted her mother to come join them outside for the langar.

It's so delicious, Ma, There's paneer and roti and dal. It is soooooo good.

George appeared at her side, and they were about to go outside when the priest came up to them. "Any jodi, any couple that comes here together, always stays together. May you both be blessed to be together forever."

They both stood still as the priest continued to bless them. He slipped his hand into hers and squeezed it. They stood there quietly for a few moments letting his blessing sink in but not saying a word out loud. Then they left to go out, and she let go of his hand.

"Come here, Ma. Come eat with us," Alina called out to them when she saw them.

As soon as they finished the langar, they were on their way to

Betaab Valley in George's Jeep. Alina talked nonstop with Suraj, not just about Vikram but about life in the valley, the food, the schools, the birds, the trees. It was as though she wanted to know every single detail and couldn't wait to learn everything about what she now thought of as her homeland.

They arrived at Betaab Valley just before the tourist buses. George rushed them all to a ticket counter to make sure they got in before the hordes made their way there.

Suraj said as he purchased tickets, "Ever since that movie, Betaab, came out, they've made this sort of a paid park. Now they charge out-of-state and foreign tourists for tickets to go in. But they won't charge me because I am local. And she is my niece, so they won't charge for Alina either."

"I'm a local now." Alina giggled. "I like that."

"I'm so happy to see you like this. This is just what I wanted," Sharmila said, but Alina had already dashed off behind Suraj, excited to see what was in store.

A local man with white doves, fluffy rabbits, and small sheep called out to them to take pictures with his animals.

"*Stop*, they are so cute." Alina was thrilled when he placed the doves on her shoulders, and she handed her phone to Suraj to take a picture. Suraj delighted in seeing his niece light up but cautioned her.

"Of course, there is no ticket, but this photo-taking is not free, not even for locals. This is how he makes his living. If we want pictures, we all have to pay."

As they came to where they could see the open space of the valley, they all stopped and stared in awe. With the mighty Lidder River rushing down the center, the large snow-capped mountains all around, willows and pine trees dancing in the winds, and wildflowers sprouting all around them, it was magical.

"Ma, this looks like a mini-Switzerland. Remember, from our trip there? It looks so similar."

George said, "I've lived here for many years and today I'm seeing this with fresh eyes. There is so much here to … fall in love with."

They came to a small bridge with bright green balustrades, leading towards a narrow path. "We have family that lives on the other side. Would you like to visit them?" Suraj asked. Before anyone else could answer, Alina was already running ahead.

"Yes. Let's go."

"I don't think I have ever seen her like this," Sharmila said to George as they walked together. A child on a bike suddenly rode in front of Sharmila, and George reached out quickly and pulled her back. She thanked him politely, and she held onto his hand and this time, she didn't let it go.

A few moments later, as they walked through the flush of green bushes and colorful flowers, they came to a large wooden house.

A light-eyed woman dressed in a bright blue pheran greeted them at the door. "We are honored that you could come. Suraj told me that you will come. I am their cousin, and this is our humble home," Archana Pandit said, welcoming them into the house.

The large room with a carved wooden ceiling smelled of freshly ground spices and jasmine incense. Tea was brewing on the small stove. Suraj made introductions and everyone sat on the floor, which was covered thickly in multicolored carpets.

The conversation flowed easily and laughter filled the room. Alina began to take selfies with everyone in the room to share with Emilio. In the selfie she took with George and her mom, she noted to herself that they were holding hands. She smiled; Emilio was right, her mom was very fond of George. She had never seen her mother hold any man's hand before. She continued taking pictures and asking Archana even more questions about local wedding customs and food and more. She made sure that Archana would attend the wedding and be part of the celebrations.

Archana served them tea and homemade biscuits as Alina chatted on and took more pictures.

Then, Archana went into a back room of the house. She returned with a pair of silver earrings.

"These are for you. For your wedding. These are traditional for a Kashmiri bride to wear. I hope you like them and will wear them for the ceremony." She placed them in Alina's hands.

"Oh, these are gorgeous. I can't take them, it's too much." Alina looked pleadingly at her mother.

"Too much? No, no, you are family. I insist." Archana gave Alina a big hug and kissed her on the forehead. "You look so much like your father did when he was young, and you have his heart—big and kind. Always be like that. Gracious with your words, generous with your love. Then you will always be your father's daughter. For him, nothing was more important than making sure people around him were happy."

The room filled with noisy children who had just come home from school. Alina took more pictures of everyone—but especially of her mother and George. With each photo, Alina felt a deep sense of happiness. Her mom, her ma, her most favorite person on the planet looked content.

"We must head to the valley now, before it gets too dark," Suraj said. A few goodbyes later, they all headed back to Betaab Valley.

In the heart of the valley, a local was offering tourists the chance to try on the traditional pherans, typical Kashmiri jewelry and headgear, and have their pictures taken. Of course, Alina couldn't resist.

Suraj left to set up the tent. He called out to them to join as soon as they finished their photo session.

George, Alina, and Sharmila all donned the outfits and took some turns posing for pictures. The local man offering the clothes insisted that they pose as if they were movie stars here on a shoot.

"You two look like Romeo and Juliet, but in an arranged marriage," Alina said as George and Sharmila posed together for a photo a bit awkwardly. Everyone laughed.

"Ah, here in the valley we would say like Sunny and Roma from the movie Betaab," the vendor said. Sharmila watched Alina pull out her phone and type something—likely the name of the movie, so she could watch it later. She smiled, knowing they'd be able to share that.

"Ma, thank you for this. And George, I'm so sorry that I was upset with you all the other day. I'm glad you found them and even happier that you're here. That *we're* here." Alina pulled them both into a hug, and Sharmila felt her shoulder bumping George's. He put his arms around Alina to return the hug, and his hand landed on Sharmila's shoulder.

A moment later, Alina was gone to take more pictures of the flowing river.

Sharmila and George sat down by the river in the open-sided tent that Suraj had set up. He was on his way to join a group of locals playing cricket by the running water. The sun was beginning to set, and the crowds had increased. All around them people were laughing and talking. Several picnickers had set up feasts on blankets laid out on the green grass.

"I have something for you," George said to Sharmila with great seriousness as he reached into a pocket of his jacket. "I've been holding onto it for the perfect moment, and I think this is it."

"What? What do you have?" Sharmila smiled coyly, if also a little anxiously.

"Here you go." George handed her a chocolate bar. "Alina told me how you gave away all your chocolate, and that it's your favorite, and I thought …"

Taking the chocolate from him, she unwrapped it, snapped a piece off, and shared it with him, then proceeded to take a big bite. "Delicious. I don't think a more perfect food has ever been created," she said.

Tourists milled around them. Vendors called out to all to come see their wares. Children ran around playing games. The cricket match now had an audience, and the whole world seemed to be celebrating just being alive in the valley.

George and Sharmila sat quietly, holding hands, each waiting for the other to say something. They moved closer to each other, still conscious of themselves and of the people around them. In a serendipitous moment, they both said in unison, "I want to say something—" The tension broke, giving way to laughter as they both allowed the symphony of shared emotions to make them feel close.

Amidst the laughter, George's eye caught hers, and he knew he could no longer resist. With tenderness, he reached out, his fingers reaching beneath Sharmila's chin. Just that one delicate touch was filled with so much longing and affection. Had the universe really conspired to bring them closer? It was a question they would ask often in the coming days.

Finally, George leaned in, and with much tenderness kissed her on the lips. The kiss seemed like a confession, like a promise, like everything they had ever needed and never allowed themselves to want.

With a hint of shyness, Sharmila gently pulled away. It was too public for her, this open area. The intimacy lingered in the air, an ache that spoke of desires yet to be fulfilled. The unspoken words hung between them as they sat quietly, still holding hands.

Under the golden glow of the setting sun, by the gentle murmur of the Lidder, Sharmila finally broke the comfortable silence that wrapped around them. "George, it's been ages since I've felt anything like this," she whispered, her voice tinged with a touch of disbelief.

George squeezed her hand in response. "I understand," he said softly, his gaze still fixed on the water. "I too thought feelings like these had long faded inside me."

Sharmila turned to face him. "I used to believe that this … this type of connection wasn't meant for me anymore. But here, with you, it's as if I've stepped into a new world. I feel like I am rediscovering something I thought I had lost forever."

George met her gaze, a gentle smile playing on his lips. "It's strange, isn't it? How we're both anchored in our pasts, yet here we are, feeling something that's so fresh, so … new."

As the sun dipped below the horizon, casting a soft blanket of twilight around them, they sat side by side, enveloped in a sense of connection that was as enigmatic as it was undeniable.

"Is this what love feels like, George?"

George was about to answer when his phone buzzed. It was a text from Wajid.

"CALL ME. IT IS URGENT."

"CAN YOU TEXT?" George replied.

"VIKRAM PANDIT'S DEATH CERTIFICATE IS MISSING. AND THERE IS MORE. CALL."

Chapter 15

George almost dropped his phone. This couldn't be happening. Not after … everything. His mind raced. He was happy about this—or was he? He wished the text had come before he'd kissed her.

He was going to lose her, he knew it. This woman who had stolen his heart with her grace, her warmth, and her amazing spirit. And yet, she wasn't his to lose. He wanted to throw his phone away, to go back in time. He didn't want to go back to Srinagar. Selfishly, he wished that text had never come. Couldn't they stay in this paradise?

"What's the matter? You look like you've seen a ghost," Sharmila said when she saw the look on his face. She squeezed his hand.

"Nothing, it's nothing," he said too quickly. *Was he so obvious?*

"Well, actually, there's a situation in Srinagar and I need to get back there right now. Can you all take a taxi back and meet me when you're done here? Is that okay? I'm sorry about this. I will talk to Suraj and make sure that you get back safely."

Sharmila looked confused. "George, is everything okay? Was it the kiss? I'm sorry. Are you upset that that happened? Was it what I said? About love? Do you not feel that way?"

"No, no. Not that at all. That kiss. Our kiss was just perfect … and love … yes, the love … but—I don't know what to tell you, I can't say anything until I go and find out more. I'm sorry. I'll text you when I get back there." Before she could ask more questions, he got up from the grass, kissed her forehead, and left.

Sharmila called his name a few times, but he didn't even turn around, just kept going.

"What happened to George?" Alina asked. She'd come back just as George rushed away and saw her mother's stunned and upset face.

"Ma, I saw you two kiss," Alina said quietly.

Sharmila blushed. She looked embarrassed and shaken. "I … I—"

"*Stop*, Ma." Alina shook her head gently. "You don't owe me an explanation. I see you with him. I see how he looks at you, and more importantly, how you look at him. I can see that you're fond of him. It makes me so happy to see you like this, Ma." She grabbed her mom's hand.

Sharmila asked Alina to sit down on the grass with her and held her daughter's hand close to her heart.

Alina said, "I have to say that at first, I wasn't sure. I noticed it, but I wasn't sure. But I like him, Ma. And as I've gotten to know him, I think he's good for you. He's good *to* you. Both Emilio and I think so."

Sharmila said nothing. She kept looking at the river. "I wonder if Vikram brought us to Kashmir to meet George? I mean, I just wonder—" The tears began to flow. Sharmila wept as she had never wept before. All the pain, all the loneliness, all the heartache began to leave her body and her spirit.

She said, "I wasn't looking, you know. I had made peace with my life. And then he came in. I just … the world seems like such a great place to be with him."

Alina hugged her mom tightly. "I know, Ma. I know. Emilio makes me feel the same. When I am with him, it is like being home. Safe and loved."

The two of them sat quietly, with the Lidder River providing a symphony of music as birds sang into the evening sky.

Finally, Sharmila spoke, breaking the silence. "I just wish he had told me where he was rushing off to. He looked so upset. I hope it isn't anything bad. Someone texted—I'm guessing it was Wajid—and George just left. I don't know how he's going to make it back there tonight. It's already late. He could have waited."

Suraj returned from his cricket match. He joined them by the river, and they ate the now-cold aloo paranthas he had packed earlier in the day. Sharmila checked her phone several times to see if George sent a message, but there was nothing. She texted him to ask if he was okay and there was no response.

Suraj hired a local taxi to take them all back to Aru Valley. It was late so they insisted that Sharmila and Alina spend the night there. Sharmila was grateful. The cottage felt snug and warm and safe.

"This culture is amazing, Ma. First, the love they show us here. Then Archana up in Betaab Valley. I mean, it is just so open-hearted. I have read so much about the difficulties that Kashmiris have experienced. I wonder if that makes them that much more open and understanding because of how much they've lost?"

Sharmila hugged her daughter tightly in response.

The next day, Suraj got them a taxi to take Sharmila and Alina back to their hotel. As soon as they arrived at the hotel, Sharmila checked at the reception desk to see if there was any news from George, but there was nothing.

"I don't know what's wrong. This is so unsettling," she kept repeating to Alina. They both sent messages to George, but neither received a reply. However, there was a message from the owner of Qayaam Gah, a resort nestled on a ridge in the Zabarwan Hills, for them to come visit, as George had set it up as a potential site for the wedding.

"We should go, Ma. Maybe George will show up there," Alina said as they climbed into bed later that night.

The next morning, their hotel arranged for a car to take them to visit Qayaam Gah. The ornate entrance that graced the resort reminded Sharmila of the old palaces she'd grown up around. The owner, whom they had met on the houseboat Sukoon, welcomed them.

"Oh, I didn't realize that you owned this as well." Alina was thrilled, as she'd enjoyed meeting him earlier. Sharmila tried to smile. "Everything will be fine, Ma, don't worry," Alina whispered to Sharmila, who seemed to be checking her phone every five seconds.

Sharmila put her phone away and decided to focus. The reason for being in Srinagar was the wedding, and now with Vikram's family attending, it was going to be even more special. She said, "We are so happy to be here and cannot wait to see this amazing property. George has been raving about it."

The owner was charming. "We are so delighted you are here, and I am happy to show you around. This is our main salon. We have seven rooms, all named for poets. First, I will show you the one that is closest to my heart. It is named for the Kashmiri poetess Habba Khatoun."

Sharmila enjoyed the tour, despite not hearing from George. She almost found herself distracted. The enchanting resort vibrated with live music as local musicians filled the air with Kashmiri songs written by Habba Khatoun and other poets. A seemingly endless outdoor infinity pool overlooked the mountains. Every part of the resort was filled with flowers and flowering trees. The wide-open jharokas, windows, overlooked the majestic mountains.

"We have a fireplace in each room and the main dining room, and our pool and outdoor spaces are heated. George told me to make sure that I told you about the fireplaces. Oh, and I know the female waza, Raahat, well. I take it you have already enjoyed her food. She caters for us sometimes."

"You spoke to George?" was the only response Sharmila could muster. She had heard his name and nothing else.

"Yes, this morning. He called to remind me about the fireplaces. I think he is going to meet you here, today, after your meal."

Sharmila was confused. Why wasn't he answering her? And now he was coming here? Well, she would ask him in person. If it was the kiss, then this was no way to behave. He was acting like a child. If he didn't want this, all he had to do was say no. Her mind ran in several directions as she wondered what to say to him.

Meanwhile, the owner of Qayaam Gah had arranged a light meal outside for the two ladies. "We will be serving you a selection of our sandwiches, desserts, and teas. I thought maybe you would like something different today," he said good-naturedly.

They sat out in the sun as a group of servers brought out plate after plate of sandwiches of every kind and teas to match. Alina tried almost everything, while Sharmila merely nibbled, waiting to see George and wondering what was wrong. Just as the desserts arrived, they heard his familiar voice talking to the resort owner.

Despite her previous decision to not to appear impatient and desperate, Sharmila rushed towards him, Alina on her heels. Even before she was in front of him, she was asking, "Where have you been? You haven't answered a single message. I've been worried sick. And look at you … What's wrong? Did something happen?"

George placed his hands on her shoulders and looked her in the eyes. She steadied, but she couldn't read his expression. With the gentlest voice and the softest tone that he could muster, he said the words that would change their worlds forever.

"Sharmila, it's about Vikram—Wajid and I have been doing some digging and there is a strong possibility that he may be alive."

Chapter 16

No one could find Sharmila. She had walked away from George and Alina the minute he broke the news to her.

"How did you know? Have you spoken with him? How do they know he is alive? Where is he? Does he remember Ma?" Alina was by his side asking a million questions a minute. She wanted to go see her father immediately.

"Alina, I don't have too many details," George said softly. Alina wasn't listening. She was leaving a voice message for Emilio sharing the news with him.

George sat down on the lawn of the resort and placed his face in his palms. "I fear I should not have said anything to your mother. Maybe she wasn't ready. I … maybe I should have said it differently."

George tried to call Sharmila again but there was no answer. She had run out of the resort dining room and he had let her. He couldn't begin to imagine how she must be feeling. He wanted to give her space but, even more, he wanted to hold her close.

"George, can I ask you something?" Alina's reaction was a mix of anticipation, anxiety, and some level of fear. "Do you think he will know who I am?"

"I'll take you as soon as we find the location where he might be. I promise. It requires so many permissions. Wajid is working on it. I'll take you both. But right now, we need to find your mother. She isn't answering her phone." George spent the next hour looking all over and around the resort. He told Alina he would take her back to the hotel so she could check there, but he had a feeling that Sharmila wouldn't be there.

The past two days had tested George. He had prayed that Wajid was simultaneously right and wrong about Vikram. Wajid's father-in-law, the diligent judge, had spent a few days looking through the paperwork to figure out why the death certificate was missing. He was about to dismiss the issue since so many papers had gone missing over the years, but a gut instinct, a feeling he had come to trust over the years, kept him going.

The answer came from one of the constables. "That bridge incident. I remember it because my father was there. He told me that they had arrested a lot of people that day. But what I do remember very clearly—I was very young, and my mother kept saying that only one person had died that day, since my father came out safe. It was a day that I have remembered every day in my life since." That was all the judge needed to get the gears of the bureaucratic machinery to churn once more. The only dead body recovered that day had been of a man named Afzal, who owned a store in the area. From everything the judge could gather, Vikram's body had never been found. There was a record that a bag with his name, some papers, a few clothes, and a painting had been recovered at the scene. It was documented that the contents of the bag had been given over to his family.

The judge started to make more inquiries. Of course, he told Wajid, the inquiries had to be discreet. There was a whole other side to this conflict in Kashmir that no one knew about.

The judge instructed his closest staff to start looking for what could have happened to Vikram Pandit. It took half a week of clearing red tape and paperwork, dead ends, and old bureaucracy, but finally they heard of a man who had been shot that day, and there were at least three eyewitnesses who mentioned that a wounded young man had been taken away from the scene by a small group of what appeared to be vigilantes.

The minute the judge heard this, he knew what could have happened to Vikram. The possibility was remote after all these years, but the judge hoped against all hope that the man would be alive and safe.

He called George and Wajid to tell them what he had found. Within an hour of his call, Wajid and George showed up in the judge's private chambers.

"Wajid, I am happy to see that your foot is out of the cast and that you are walking again," the judge said, then asked the two of them to sit down.

"I will try to explain this the best way that I can. I am telling you again that there is no guarantee that Vikram is alive. But if he is, I think I know where he will be." With a deep breath, he began to tell them a tale that was bizarrely frightening and yet so filled with hope.

In the early nineties, a lot of Kashmiris were being killed. While there were many who moved—or were relocated by the government—to other areas outside Kashmir, there were those who were left behind and were being slaughtered by the terrorist organizations. At the same time, a small, super-secret underground group came into being. Their name was Nyay (Justice). The judge told the two bewildered men that Nyay was responsible for hiding a lot of Kashmiris who were at risk of being killed by the terrorists. While Nyay provided a safe haven for people being targeted by terrorists, there was a catch. Once they rescued someone, that person could never leave the organization. This was done for their own safety, that of their families, and now the safety of all the others who were hiding in Nyay facilities.

"In Vikram's case, as we pieced the case together, I think what happened is Vikram saw his friend's body and ran to help thinking that his friend may still be alive. This part is substantiated by witnesses. We know that he was then shot. My hypothesis is that he recognized his terrorist shooters. If this was the case, and I believe it to be so, then the next part makes sense," said the judge, explaining that witnesses had seen some people take away the wounded young man.

"That would make sense," Wajid said. "I have heard of Nyay. George, it is like what Daneen told me about DC—the underground railroad in the olden days of strife there."

George shook his head, but he wasn't convinced. "This is a long shot. I appreciate your theory but, I mean, it has been almost thirty years. If he was safe, then why has he not contacted his family? I don't know. This is an interesting theory."

The judge took off his glasses and cleaned them with a small white cloth.

"I love skeptics. I am one myself. But in this case, I can tell you why they don't come out and reclaim their families, George. Would you like to hear about it or see it?" The judge had an annoyed tinge to his voice.

"I don't follow? See it?"

"Yes, my man. See it. Would you like to see it?" the judge asked again, this time standing up and banging his hands on his table for effect.

George looked taken aback. Before he could say anything, the judge was summoning his clerk and asking him to bring files from almost a decade earlier, calling out the files by the years, not by names.

"Now, I want you to see this." The judge opened the first file and spilled out the contents on the table in front of George and Wajid.

The pictures on the table were graphic and disturbing. Images of corpses with limbs torn off, of women being tortured and children in body bags.

"Do you see this? This is what would happen to the families of the people who saw and reported the terrorists. We know of at least two people who left the shelter of Nyay and reported what had happened to them and identified the terrorists. They were never found again, and their families … well, you see it in front of you."

George got up and excused himself. He went to the small public bathroom in the courthouse and threw up. The images were gory and shook him. He tried to steady himself against the sink. Finally, he splashed cold water on his face, cleaned himself the best he could, and went back into the judge's chambers.

"I'm so sorry. I had no idea. I know little about that part of Kashmir's history since Daneen and I left here decades ago."

"Aba, father, tell us what we can do to find Vikram Pandit," Wajid said. "His family is here now, and I know it is safe. In fact, you yourself had told me that the government is providing safe haven for people who had gone into hiding and is protecting their families now."

The judge nodded. "I have made a few calls and we have a few places that you can go and check. We cannot send the police there. And my people cannot go. The information is that Vikram is alive and is at one of these places. I can provide you the addresses, and if you or his family want to go and check, then it is possible that you will find him."

George asked for the addresses.

"It is safe for you all to go there. But I can tell you—it will be painful if you find him, and painful if you don't." The judge's stance had softened and he offered some sage words. He told them to go work with an officer named Prakash Sarkar who was known to have good connections with Nyay, and who could, if he agreed, help them in locating where Vikram might be. Then he added, as gently as he could, "I hope you will prepare his family before taking this task on. People change in thirty years. The man that they knew and loved may or may not be the same person now."

"I can't even imagine. All I know is that if I had lost Daneen and there was even a one percent chance that I could see her again, I would take it." George took the addresses, thanked the judge profusely, and decided to tell Sharmila. Then together with her he would go find the true love of her life, Vikram Pandit.

Chapter 17

The late afternoon breeze was cold, and the songbirds appeared to have gone into hibernation in anticipation of the cold winter months ahead. The waters of Dal Lake looked icy in the last shards of the early November sun.

It had been many hours since George first told Sharmila about Vikram, and she was still not answering her phone. He had not found her on the grounds of Qayaam Gah, nor anywhere nearby. George knew that he needed to find Sharmila and get Alina to calm down.

Alina was on the phone with Emilio, complaining at the top of her voice. "I can't understand my mother's reaction. She just ran away, Emilio. Who does that? Isn't she happy that my father may be alive?" She wipes her eyes.

"Emilio, I don't understand. What do you mean, 'Give her time'? My father could be alive. George is going to go look for her. I am so angry with her. What is wrong with her?" Alina was wiping her eyes.

George signaled to her to get into the Jeep, and they began driving to their hotel in hopes that Sharmila had gone there. The entire way, Alina alternated between talking to Emilio, who was just starting his school day in the US, and calling her mother's cellphone. At one point, she put Emilio on speaker. "You know, Alina, your mother has found a companion in George. A man, you yourself told me, who's good for her. Now this. Just when the poor woman seems to finally have found love, this happens."

Alina quickly took him off the speaker and hoped that George hadn't heard all that. "That is not fair on her part. My dad comes first." Alina hung up the phone. As soon as they reached the hotel, George asked Alina to check to see if Sharmila was in the room.

He waited outside as he texted Sharmila's phone, begging her to call him. When his phone rang, it was Alina informing him that her mother wasn't there and, according to the front desk, had not come in at all that day.

"I am going to look for her. You stay here in case she comes back," he told her, and drove towards Dal Lake. He thought she could be there, as she loved it so much. It took him a long time to get there in the midst of the evening traffic. But there was no sign of her. He parked his Jeep and looked all around the main docks of the lake, showed as many vendors as he knew her picture, and he asked if they had seen her. None had.

He called Wajid. "I am texting you her picture. Can you ask your contacts at the Shankaracharya Temple to see if she is there? I will text you other locations I took them to. Maybe she went to one of them?"

George went to Lal Chowk, then all the nearby gardens, the markets, and other places they'd been to. By now, it was nearing eleven o'clock at night, and there was still no sign of Sharmila. Wajid reported that none of the other tour guides had seen her.

George began to panic. He cursed himself that he should have been more gentle with her, or maybe should have told Vikram's brother first. Then he wondered if she went to Aru Valley. He called Suraj and tried to talk casually about the wedding. He surmised that she wasn't there, or Suraj would surely have said something.

Then it occurred to him. There was only one place that he hadn't checked.

George rushed home to his houseboat.

She was sitting outside the boat with her face buried in her hands. He could tell that she had been crying. He quickly texted Alina to say he had found Sharmila and that she should not worry.

"You found me. Sorry I haven't returned any calls or messages," she said as she felt him sitting down with her. She wiped her tears and looked straight ahead, avoiding making eye contact with him. "How did you know I would be here?"

"I thought that if I were you, where could I go where only one person could find me?"

She began to cry uncontrollably again.

"Have you met him? Is he okay? He was shot. Does he remember me? Did he ask about the baby? Did he look okay? Was he healthy? Was he okay? I don't even know if I am asking the right questions, or what I am supposed to ask." Her questions came one after the other. He could feel her slipping through his fingers.

"It's cold out here, Sharmila, and you are shivering. Why don't we go inside? I will answer all your questions as best as I can."

She sat at the tiny dining table, and he began to make some kahwa. Slowly he related all that had happened, how Vikram had been carried off by the Nyay group, and how after all these years he could still be in danger from the terrorists who shot him.

***

Wajid's father-in-law had told him that a police officer who had been instrumental in helping the Nyay group was Prakash Sarkar. Wajid and George had rushed over to try to meet with Officer Sarkar, but it was nearly impossible, even with the informal request from the judge. The officer was simply too busy, they were told by his staff. They spent several hours trying to argue with them, but to no avail.

George kept thinking that he had heard the name before—Sarkar. Then it clicked. That was the last name of the wedding planner, the same wedding planner Sharmila had originally hired. That morning, when they were arguing about his poor wedding planning, Rami Sarkar had threatened them, mentioning that his brother was a bigwig with the local police and could throw them in jail.

"Wajid, you go home and wait. I'll let you know when—or if—you should meet me back here." George rushed out. A quick search on his phone told him that Mr. Rami's office was in the southern part of the Lal Chowk. He zoomed over in his Jeep, hoping and praying that Mr. Rami was there.

"You. I remember you. That Kashmiri man with you stole my client. What do you want? Get out of here." Mr. Rami would have none of it. "You people think you can steal from me. No, you cannot. I was right. I told everyone you will come crawling back and here you are. Crawling back to me."

George let him go on for a few minutes, then began to tell him what was going on. He literally began to beg Mr. Rami for help. "Can you please call your brother? Please? Even if I can see him for just a few minutes. We need some help. Please?"

Mr. Rami was adamant, but eventually George appealed to his wedding planner side. "Just think—Vikram Pandit is possibly alive and well and thriving. Now, this estranged father should be able to give his daughter away at the wedding. Can you please assist?"

Mr. Rami stopped arguing and his eyes softened.

"Please, Mr. Rami. This is not for me or for Wajid. This is for that family. One call from you could make that family whole again. It can give Sharmila the love of her life back and Alina her father."

"You know, you are a smart man. You know you are." Mr. Rami called his brother and within an hour George and Wajid found themselves seated across from Officer Sarkar, a tall, dominating, and powerful man. He listened patiently to what George had to say and quietly contemplated their request.

"It is not easy to find the locations of Nyay. It isn't like they publish these addresses. The judge did call me after I heard from my brother. Those addresses the judge has are old and useless. I do have some information on their new location. But, again, I am not sure. Many of the people they held have been coming out of hiding as the new government is helping them." The police officer was succinct, to the point, and sharp. "Finding him won't be easy, I can tell you that. And if you do, he may not want to come out of hiding. I am just telling you. People who go through this change—the change is dramatic and, sadly, many times not very pleasant."

He handed over two addresses and let them go with this caution. "I am giving you these addresses as you came in through the judge, a man I trust and respect. My brother didn't have nice things to say about the two of you, but then he doesn't like anyone."

George and Wajid waited, as it seemed like there was more to come.

"I want only two people to go. Wajid, you, and take the lady, what did you say her name was? Sharmila? Yes, her. No other man. Certainly not a white man. Go in simple clothes. You will be searched. I will call ahead. I am giving you my card. Show them the card. I wish you success."

That had been the last conversation.

***

"Wajid is ready to take you tomorrow," George said. Halfway through talking to her he had switched his drink from tea to whisky.

Barely above a whisper, Sharmila said, "I am scared. Do you think he will want to be found?"

"I don't know. But if I lost someone like you, I know I would want to be found."

"Life does this to me. Never asks. Just changes everything without any warning," Sharmila said as tears filled her eyes again. He leaned over, wiped her tears, and kissed her hands. They sat together watching the moon in the distance as the boat rocked gently.

"Would you like me to drop you back at the hotel?" George asked her.

"No. If it is okay with you, I would just like to be here with you."

They spent the night sitting on the couch in the main room of the houseboat. She placed her head on his lap, and he ran his fingers through her hair until she fell asleep. He wiped his own tears and fell asleep sitting on the couch.

This was not how he had imagined them spending their first night alone together.

Everything had indeed changed.

Chapter 18

The next morning, Sharmila waited inside George's houseboat for Wajid to show up. She had spent the early part of the morning on the phone calming Alina down and telling her Wajid was going to take her to find Vikram. Alina, as usual, had been insistent on coming. But she finally let it go when Sharmila explained the danger it could pose to them and possibly to Vikram.

"You haven't touched your breakfast. Can you at least eat one piece of toast?" George asked. Sharmila sat down to eat. She could barely swallow and used gulps of water to get the buttered toast down.

"George, I want to say something … about you and me," Sharmila said, and he quickly got up from the dining table and turned his back to her, pretending to make more toast.

"There is nothing to say. I understand. It is about you and Vikram." His voice was cracking.

"I need to tell you something. It is what I have been thinking since you told me about finding him. Please." Sharmila was about to say more when there was a knock on the door. It was Wajid, ready to take her to locate Vikram.

Wajid walked in, still limping on his ankle. His skin carried the natural fairness of his mountain heritage, contrasting with his dark black hair and a well-groomed goatee.

"Good morning, Sharmila. I have to say that this has never happened on any other tours I have conducted. Now I just have to take you on this journey one hobble at a time," said Wajid, making a feeble attempt to lighten the tense atmosphere in the room.

Sharmila got up slowly and called out to George again. He turned around to face her. She stepped towards him and gave him a tight hug and abruptly turned and left with Wajid.

"The first location, surprisingly, is quite near," Wajid told her. "I thought that these underground groups used to hide in the different valleys around Kashmir, but this one is here in Srinagar. My guess is that now that it is safer, a lot of them are coming back into the city." Wajid had a small car and Sharmila kept turning around, looking at the last glimpses of George standing on the deck of the houseboat.

"Sharmila? Are you listening?"

"I worry that this is too sudden. That this is almost too much of a lucky break. I am almost afraid to be happy, Wajid. Does that make any sense?" The houseboat disappeared from sight and the little car made its way to the north end of Srinagar.

"Well, you got unlucky in a minute too, right? So why is some sudden good luck to be questioned? You know, George always tells me to open my perspective and that if I do that, life will surprise me. I offer you the same advice." Wajid turned the car into small lanes and bylanes, looking for the first address that the officer had provided. He placed a hand on his jacket pocket to ensure that he still had the officer's card. It was there.

Sharmila was fielding frantic calls from Alina and telling her to stay put and be strong, and that everything would be all right very soon.

It took about an hour of asking questions of random strangers on the street to find the place.

As the car wound its way up the serpentine path to the rustic house, the scent of apple trees wafted through the air, mingling with memories of forgotten loves and lives. The house, Wajid informed her, used to belong to a Kashmiri millionaire.

"This was his manor, centuries ago, when the valley was a crossroads of cultures and empires, a place where merchants from the Silk Road rested their weary feet." The storyteller and tour guide part of Wajid took over for the moment. "This home has witnessed an amazing amount of history, from the sixteenth century time of the Mughal emperors to the era of British colonialism. Well, and then to the terror that tore us apart."

Now it sheltered a community of souls who could not choose the path they wanted but hid here for the safety of their loved ones and their own lives.

"There it is," Wajid said. Sharmila tried to see the building. Nestled deep in the woods off this secluded road was a large decrepit house that whispered tales of a bygone era. Sharmila could see how the group that lived there had made an effort to shield it from the clamor of the main roads.

"It even looks like a sanctuary for lost souls," she said quietly as she felt her eyes brimming with tears and her hands shaking. She couldn't tell if it was fear or anticipation or both.

The house, with its timeworn wooden façade, was covered in wildflowers and all kinds of vegetation. The greens hugged it as though they were holding secrets of the faceless, nameless many that it had housed. If there had been any paint on the outer walls, it had faded to a muted ochre. The roof seemed to sag under the weight of broken dreams.

The grounds of the house were populated by sheep and small children playing with wooden toys. Sharmila could see two men working in the vegetable garden to the side of the house. She peered and stared to see if one of them was Vikram. *It has been a few decades—will I even recognize him?*

"There is no security? This seems too easy," she whispered to Wajid.

"Oh, no. Don't let that fool you. Look to the right. There are three men with rifles in the back and they are pointed straight at us. The officer told me that he had given them my car number and a picture of each of us. It is the only reason we are still alive."

As soon as he stopped his car, the men with the rifles came into full view. Without a word, Wajid reached into his pocket and showed them Officer Sarkar's card. They moved aside and let him and Sharmila step out of the car. They were both unceremoniously patted down and let into the house.

Within the house's dimly lit interiors, the walls, adorned with faded tapestries and aging photographs, contrasted with the strong smell of freshly brewing saffron tea and cinnamon-laced meat curry. Wajid and Sharmila saw a group of women sitting in the center of the room, talking and knitting. The open windows brought in the crisp mountain air. It was as though the elements of the present were fighting with the history of the place, desperately trying to imbue some hope and some brightness into the darkest corners of the house and the history its residents bore.

"Come in. Sit. Please." An older woman got up and motioned for them to be seated on the colorful rug at the center of the room. The group quieted down. Before Wajid or Sharmila could speak, she said, "You are looking for Vikram Pandit? What do you know about him? Why are you looking for him? You are his family?"

Wajid motioned to Sharmila, who began to speak hesitatingly about Vikram, his paintings, their short time together, their daughter, and his family in Aru Valley. And finally, about Alina's upcoming wedding.

"I see." The old woman seemed deep in thought. Then she called out to one of the men holding a rifle to come in. She whispered something in his ear. He nodded and answered in an equally quiet voice and left the room.

In the meantime, Sharmila could see messages on her phone from Alina, and she could almost bet everything that the buzzing in Wajid's phone was from George.

When the old woman spoke again, her voice was firm. "Yes, there was a Vikram Pandit amongst us. But I am not sure he is the one you are looking for. He was not a painter, but a gardener."

"Oh, I see," Sharmila said and added, "I only have a picture of him from when he was a young man. Can I show you that? Maybe that will help?"

Sharmila opened her phone and showed them a photo of the picture that Vikram's mother had shown Alina.

Several of the women in the group came up and took a look. The old woman stared at the picture and said, "Maybe, I can't be sure. My memory isn't what it used to be."

One of the other women spoke up. "I know him," she said.

"He is the one. The gardener. But he isn't here now. He was moved about ten years or so ago to another location. I have the address. If you want, you can go there and see."

The woman hadn't even finished speaking when Sharmila began to cry. The tears did not stop. The man whom she had spent half her life with through memories was alive, and here. He was breathing the same air. She couldn't believe it.

Wajid reached over and placed his hand on her shoulder and answered a call on his phone with a simple. "Yes, we believe he is alive and in Kashmir."

Sharmila and Wajid thanked the group and returned to his car.

"Where is the other address, Wajid? Can we go now? Or is it too far?"

Wajid sat quietly. "Sharmila, this place. I know of it. It is called Khauf-e-Asmaan, the terror from the sky. I have never been. It is about five hours from here. We can go, but we will need to be prepared. We need the Jeep, and I will need to tell Officer Sarkar about this. This can be very risky."

"If he is alive and here, I need to find him. We need to go today. Now. Will we reach it by nightfall? Can we get a rental? Let's do it right now."

"Yes, it is as Tagore said: 'You can't cross the sea merely by standing and staring at the water.' So we do need to go." Wajid pulled out his phone and called Officer Sarkar.

Chapter 19

Within an hour of getting permission and the Jeep, Sharmila and Wajid began the journey to Khauf-e-Asmaan. The first part of the journey went through the heart of Srinagar and the bustling markets. Then as the sun began to set, darkness draped the treacherous, unpaved roads leading them outside Srinagar to their perilous destination. After about two hours of twists and turns and maze-like roads, they ended up on a narrow, hilly road snaking its way through dense forests. A full moon had risen, and looming pine trees and thick underbrush cast long, haunting shadows along the road.

Neither spoke until Wajid stopped the Jeep so that they could stretch and eat some food he had picked up.

"I worry about George and what this will do to him," he said without being asked.

"What?" Sharmila turned to him, surprised.

"When my sister died, George broke down. He felt so responsible for her death," Wajid said as he sat on the grass.

Sharmila just listened.

"I could not bear the thought of him breaking down alone in the US. So, I convinced him to come here. For years, even after coming here, he seemed like a ghost. He sat in that houseboat and drank and wept and slept. I can't remember a single time that he actually laughed."

Sharmila could feel there was something coming that involved her.

"Please, would you like more tea?" Wajid asked instead. She nodded and he added some more tea to her plastic cup.

Wajid told her to get back in the Jeep. They continued to brave the rugged terrain, but even the sturdy wheels of the Jeep grappled with the uneven, rocky path. The air grew colder as they ventured deeper into the wilderness.

The Jeep slowed as the vegetation on either side of the road seemed to take over, the overgrown branches clawing at the vehicle, creating a disconcerting sense of entrapment. Suddenly Wajid braked hard as a big animal ran out of the darkness across in front of them.

As they watched the animal — it looked like a deer — disappear into the brush, Wajid said, "It was only about a year ago that George came out of his darkness. It was when he started touring the valley with me. He began to smile and be involved with life again," Wajid said. "And now, I worry. I see him happy. You will go on with your life with Vikram. But my George, my brother. What of him?"

There were no more words exchanged on the topic for the rest of the trip.

They continued despite the fallen trees that blocked their path. The Jeep's engine grumbled in protest against the high-altitude conditions, while a dense fog enveloped them, rendering visibility a mere illusion as the headlights reflected off the mist.

All other topics were forgotten as doubt crept into their minds, fueled by the unsettling stories Wajid had told Sharmila about their destination earlier. "I never knew that this place could be associated with the underground Nyay group. It has only ever been rumored to be a place of ill fate and tragedy—the most famous one being how many wildfires suddenly seem to start up there with no explanation."

Sharmila checked her phone. There was no service. "If we get stuck here, what's going to happen?"

Wajid turned the Jeep off the path as they came upon a tiny, paved road to the left.

"We cannot continue in this fog. I will park here for the night. We should be safe in the Jeep. We can take turns sleeping. We can start again in the morning. Okay?"

Sharmila nodded, though she was terrified. She wished George were with them. She worried about Alina. She wondered what Vikram would be like, how he would react to her. The thought of him giving his daughter away at the wedding and participating in the rituals actually made her smile. She wanted Alina to have a good relationship with her father—and she could hardly believe that it was a possibility now.

"Here," Wajid said, giving her a couple of thick blankets. He told her to get some sleep, saying he would wake her in a few hours to take over the watch.

Neither of them really slept.

Finally the sun was up, and the morning's tentative light gave them the incentive they needed to continue.

They finished the remaining tea, which was now cold despite being in the thermos.

"There it is." This time it was Sharmila who saw the house—or what once could have been a house. It didn't look like there was any life there. The forest around it had burnt to the ground. There was no wild vegetation, no garden, no animals, no birds, no signs of life.

"What is happening here, Wajid?"

Wajid simply shrugged.

"I would have bet my life that this place didn't exist, but I guess it does. I wonder if I can do a ghost tour of Kashmir?" Wajid said, and instantly regretted his joke. "Sorry, bad timing. I am just nervous about being here."

"No, no, don't apologize. I feel bad that I have pulled you and George into my messy life. I am so sorry." Sharmila worried about what they were going to find here.

"No, no, *I'm* sorry. George and I are happy to help you. Once you came here and with us, you became family," he said good-naturedly. "Now, let's see what is happening here."

With caution and curiosity, they ventured closer. Wajid looked around for men with rifles, for any signs of life. There didn't seem to be anyone around.

"Stop. Stop right there or we will shoot."

The booming voice came from within the house. Wajid and Sharmila stopped in their tracks, frozen.

"We are here with permission from Officer Sarkar," Wajid called. "I am Wajid, and this is Sharmila. He said he called here to let you know."

"Does this look like a place that accepts calls, you fool?" an old voice responded with a touch of laughter.

An old man with a larger-than-normal walking stick walked

out of the manor. Behind him were about six other old men. One of them had a knife, but it didn't look like anyone else was armed.

"Sir, we are here in peace. We are looking for a man. A family member. That is all." Wajid's voice was shaking. "For Vikram Pandit. We are looking for Vikram Pandit."

"Then you are in the right place," the old man replied.

Chapter 20

As soon as Sharmila and Wajid entered the hotel room, Alina all but pounced on her mother. "*Ma!* You haven't answered a single call or text. George and I have been worried out of our minds. Ma, what happened? Why didn't he come with you? Did he know about me? Did he recognize you?"

Sharmila looked past Alina to see George. He sat on the couch, his face creased with deep concern. He opened his mouth to say something but stopped. Sharmila dropped into a chair by the table, and Wajid sat down on the other end of the couch as he winced from the pain in his ankle acting up.

"Please send up tea service for four. And two orders of samosas and some pakoras, please." George looked worried as he spoke to room service, and motioned to Alina to get Sharmila and Wajid some water and give them a minute to catch their breath before pelting them with more questions.

Alina sprang into action. In addition to water, she gave Wajid a pill for the pain and brought both of them damp towels from the bathroom so they could freshen up. Neither of them looked like they were ready to share anything.

"Ma, what is happening? Your eyes are so swollen. What is going on?"

Looking exhausted and forlorn, Sharmila took a deep breath and began to speak slowly. She related how they couldn't find him in the first place and ended up at the second safe house.

"I guess we found him, but not in a way that we wanted," Wajid added.

"What is that supposed to mean? Is he suffering from an illness? Did he not remember you?" Alina was exasperated, while George just sat quietly and listened.

Sharmila looked at Wajid with sad eyes. He nodded.

"So, the old man who watches over the safe house told us that Vikram had lived there on and off for years. He had many mental issues after the incident at the bridge. The man said he wanted to leave at first, to go be with his family but …" Sharmila felt the bile rise in her throat.

"It is an ugly part of our history as humans," Wajid said. "Vikram heard about and saw the slaughter of men and women who tried to go back to their villages. He soon understood he was a marked man, a sort of walking corpse, in the words of the old man."

Alina placed her hand on her heart. "I can't even imagine what his life must have been like."

Sharmila looked steadily into Alina's widened eyes. "Alina, your father was alive till a few months ago. He was being moved from one safe house to another. On the way there was an accident, and no one survived. The old man who met us had performed Vikram's last rites and spread his ashes over the land behind the house there."

Sharmila's eyes were empty and her words came out slowly. Wajid tried to add some details, but he could barely speak.

There was painful silence in the room, until Sharmila tried to say what she thought would ease some of the deep pain. "In a way, I am relieved he lived in a safe place for many years."

"Are you going to call his mother?" Alina asked. "Of course, you must be happy he's dead, right, Ma? So now you can do whatever the hell you want." Alina stormed out of the room.

Sharmila got up to go after her, but George rose too. "Wait. She is just upset. Let me go get her."

"No, no. You both stay here. I will make sure she is okay," Wajid offered. He left the room just as the room service waiter came in with the order. Sharmila managed to control herself until the waiter left.

"Do you think she is right? Do you think I am that evil that I wanted him to be dead so that I could be with the man I love now?" Sharmila couldn't hold back the anger in her voice. "After everything I have done for her, loved her, left everything for her, this child? This child doubts her mother's integrity?"

George cleared his throat. "She's just upset. All this is very stressful. Things have been up and down since she got here. She is still young. You know she loves you. She will come around."

Sharmila went to the window to take one last look at the scenic mountains outside the room.

"And you? What about you? You don't think I have integrity either, do you?"

"How are you getting that?" George looked surprised and upset.

Sharmila turned on him, her eyes a complex storm of emotions that raged within her.

"I think I told you that I had made peace with the fact that my life with Vikram was over. I loved him with all my heart, and his memory is sacred. But when I opened up to you and told you how I felt, I don't think you understood that."

George stayed quiet for a minute. "Sharmila, it was hard. I wondered what I would have done if Daneen came back. I thought you would want to be with him. That you were still longing for him. I couldn't compete with that. I don't want to."

Sharmila shook her head. "That is where we are different. I yearned for Vikram to be alive when you came and told me that there was a chance. Not for me, but for Alina. My love for him has—I don't know how to explain it—I suppose it has transformed into a deep, enduring affection and a longing for him to be a part of Alina's life."

"I don't know what I would have done if it was Daneen and there was a chance that she was still alive." George tried to be open, but his voice was quivering with uncertainty, even anger.

"You think I am this fickle? When I told you how I felt, do you think that was because of just circumstance? You think my love for you would change if there was any other man on the scene?"

George leaned back, reining in his own emotions. "I didn't say that," he replied, defensive. "But it's natural to have doubts, isn't it? We haven't known each other for very long."

She stood up, her anger flaring. "Doubts? You doubt my love for you?"

He rose to his feet as well, his frustration mirroring hers. "No, it's not about doubting your love. It's about trust. Trust takes time to build."

She paced back and forth, the tension in the room palpable.

"Trust? Is that what this is about? You think I'd just run back to him at the first chance?"

He shook his head, his voice strained. "No, I just—"

She cut him off, her voice rising. "I've waited over twenty years for him to come back, and he never did. I moved on, found happiness with you. My heart belongs to you now. I never felt this way for anyone else. But if you doubt it, then perhaps we aren't right for each other."

"I'm sorry, I am just being honest."

Tears welled in her eyes as she looked at him, her anger giving way to vulnerability. "I thought you would understand. I thought you knew how much you mean to me. I cannot be with someone who doesn't trust my love for them."

Still crying, Sharmila asked George to leave.

The next morning, a heartbroken Sharmila and an irritable Alina abruptly packed their bags and left Kashmir to return to Washington, DC.

Chapter 21

Five months later
Washington, DC

Sharmila double-checked her list. All the wedding trousseau, the gifts for the guests, her own outfits, sandals … the list was two pages long.

She put the list down and sat at the dining table. The last few months had exhausted her, or perhaps aged her—she couldn't tell the difference. She pressed the tips of each finger on her hand trying to calm her nerves. Then, despite the pain and the exhaustion, she smiled to herself. Her daughter, the light of her life, was getting married, and everything had worked out beautifully for the wedding.

Emilio's call brought her out of her reverie.

"Emilio, how are you, my dear? Have you checked on the visas? Passports? Tickets?" It felt like the hundredth time she was peppering him with questions, but she couldn't help it.

Ever patient, Emilio responded sweetly, "Yes, we're ready. Are you? The flight is delayed, which is why I'm calling. We'll still get there in time, so don't worry."

Sharmila hung up and turned back to her list. Normally, a delayed flight would have caused some agitation, but not this week. So much good news! Alina had been accepted to her top-choice nursing school. Emilio's entire family—including his now-healthy nonna—would all be coming to Srinagar for the wedding. Her sister, finally out of the silent retreat she had been on, had confirmed that she would be there as well. Everything was falling into place.

She was proud that she could pay for it all. When Alina was a baby she had struggled to support the two of them, so she eventually—and reluctantly—relied on her family's trust fund. But once her paintings started to sell, she used her own money. She painted, she taught, she gave lectures—anything to help her and Alina stay independent. And miraculously, in the past few months three of her most recent paintings had sold for exorbitant amounts. Then a highly complimentary newspaper article announcing the auction results had referred to her as "a charming painter who is just discovering her potential."

She only occasionally thought about George—mostly when she was painting. She tried to keep those thoughts occasional, but that had become more difficult as the wedding approached. When Alina had shared her intention to invite him, Sharmila just smiled at her daughter and said nothing. Alina had a loving relationship with him, and she wouldn't stand in the way of that. She told herself she didn't want to see him. But as she made her plans to travel back to India, it was harder and harder to believe that.

Sharmila shook off her feelings and went to her painting

studio. The art-filled room was on the top-most floor of her quaint townhouse that overlooked the Potomac River. As always, all her worries, anxieties, and pain were forgotten for the moment. This was her sanctuary, where her emotions were laid bare on canvas, freeing her spirit and her heart. She kept the brochure that the auction house had sent her in there, with images of her three sold paintings inside it. If anyone—particularly Alina—had seen the references to George in the paintings, they hadn't mentioned it.

Sharmila's studio, once a lively haven of color and warmth, now reflected her quiet solitude. While she was thrilled that Alina was getting married, there was a part of her that was grieving—Sharmila would be fully alone for the first time in her life. There was a time this wouldn't have bothered her—not much—but now "alone" meant something different.

She could admit it now, if only to herself. She missed George. A lot. The distance between them hadn't eased the ache of her heart as she had hoped.

Picking up the brochure, Sharmila ran her fingers over the images of the paintings she had poured her heart into, every stroke telling the story of their love. Colorful shikaras and vivid Himalayan sunsets over Dal Lake melted into the canvas like liquid gold, capturing the warmth of their moments together. The Shankaracharya temple painting showed the temple radiant under a full moon. Hidden amidst the vibrant landscapes were subtle hints of George—a shadowy figure, his silhouette in the moonlight.

"Ma! I'm home, are you ready?" Alina called. In the studio she placed her arms around her mother's waist. "I cannot wait to go back to Srinagar. Wajid and Suraj Uncle have been calling nonstop. All the details are final. But you know me, I will have to go and see."

Sharmila smiled. "You know, when I see your face now, I can see what my mother used to say about brides. You have the roop now, the bridal glow. Makes my heart so happy, my child."

"Oh, before I forget!" Alina said. "Do you remember that red pashmina shawl you bought me? I meant to tell you that I've been in touch with them, and I have a wonderful present for you too, Ma. From Emilio and me. A custom shawl that I think you will love." Before Sharmila could respond, Alina kissed her on the forehead and went outside to call Emilio.

"Emilio, she looks so sad. Maybe I should tell her."

"No, no," Emilio said. "Don't worry. Everything will be okay. Now listen to me: we have a few more things left to do."

Emilio gave her a list of final arrangements to make, including calling the owner of the Qayaam Gah resort to ensure that all would go as planned. She did what was on the list, then went back to her room to check her luggage and get dressed for the trip back to her parents' homeland. Her mind kept wandering over the last few months. She had noticed distinct changes in her mother's moods and, more importantly, the more subtle changes in her art that Sharmila had tried to hide. But Alina could clearly see Sharmila's heartbreak bleeding onto the canvas, raw and unfiltered. Her new paintings were beautiful but had subdued energy about them. Alina had tried to coax her mother into speaking of her emotions, but Sharmila remained stoic, brushing away her daughter's concern with a faint smile.

Alina wished she could do something. She felt partially

responsible for her mother's heartbreak. If only she had not been angry with her regarding her father. If only she had at least made an effort to get her and George to talk. There were so many *if onlys*. If only it wasn't too late. But then she thought—maybe it wasn't.

Last night, at a final dinner with Emilio's family, Sharmila and his mom walked in with the pasta, all ready to eat.

"Ma, that looks fantastic," Alina said. "Speaking of fantastic food—Raahat just sent over the menu. I spoke to her this morning and she said George had been over and helped her decide on the final menu."

Sharmila just nodded.

Emilio tried to give her a look, but Alina ignored him. "And the flowers are finalized—George worked with Zarina on that too. Now all we need to do—"

"Alina," Sharmila said gently. "Let's talk about you and Emilio, shall we?" She nodded at Emilio's family and lifted her glass. "After all, it's your wedding."

Alina and Emilio exchanged glances, hers an apology, and his *I told you so*. He texted her while everyone ate dinner in silence. "Your mama is totally in love." Alina smiled to herself, because he was right. And hopefully, if all went well, everyone else would know that, too.

Chapter 22

A Few Days Later
Qayaam Gah, Kashmir

Orange marigolds, white chrysanthemums, and deep magenta roses adorned Qayaam Gah. Zarina, the flower vendor from Dal Lake, had found tulips in what seemed every possible color and used them in varying combinations throughout the resort. Despite a light early spring chill, the resort had a warm vibe. Radiant lighting highlighted every corner. Small golden chandeliers hung all around and brought warmth to the main salon.

Sharmila had specifically asked Zarina to create centerpieces that were a reflection of the bride's unwavering commitment and the groom's steadfast promise. Using that as her guide, Zarina had created remarkably thoughtful centerpieces for every table. They had the rustic allure of dried wooden bark paired with the delicate charm of fresh lotus petals. "Just like the couple—so different, and yet so perfect together," she said. The graceful silhouette of the painstakingly preserved bark signified, she told them, strength and commitment of seasons gone by. The bark was covered with delicate wisps of soft lotus petals that appeared to be dancing. The petals, she said, brought hope and joy for the present and future.

What truly set the centerpieces apart was the touch no one expected. Zarina had placed tiny crystals on top of the petals, like dewdrops. The crystals caught the soft illumination of the chandeliers, the fireplace, and the starlight, and cast a soft glow on the tables.

While Suraj and Wajid had helped Alina make the final arrangements, many details had been taken care of by the owner of the resort. Over the last few months, he had worked with Alina by phone, text, and email to ensure that she would be happy with it all. Now Alina was back in Kashmir, and yes, very pleased.

"How is the food preparation coming along?" Alina asked Suraj. He had stepped in to be Alina's on-site assistant to help take care of the wedding preparations. He had become quite fond of his niece and was delighted to help.

"Raahat is here, and she and her staff have been cooking all day. I will check in with her in a few minutes. Don't you think you should be going to get dressed? I can take care of all the details."

"Yeah, yeah, I'll go soon," Alina said. "The makeup lady keeps calling me. But I just wanted to make sure. Emilio is outside ensuring that the paths are all clear for the guests. There was snow this morning. But I should go in before he sees me, or it's bad luck," Alina added, laughing.

Music filled the air as the musicians seated at the far end of the room began to test out their instruments to ensure that they would be ready for the ceremony.

Alina saw Wajid out of the corner of her eye. He was busy helping the priest set up the mandap, the main area where the wedding would take place. The mandap was covered with a red carpet that Alina had chosen earlier that week. She had seen it and instantly fallen in love, demanding they find a place to include it in the wedding. The columns that surrounded the platform were wrapped with fragrant jasmine flower garlands.

"Wajid, have you seen George?" Alina asked casually, hoping against hope that George would at least listen to reason and end this cold war with Sharmila.

"Yes, I have seen him, and I passed on your message to him. He didn't say yes but he didn't say no either. Keep the faith, Alina. George has always done the right thing. And I know he will this time, too."

"I hope you are right, and he will come. That will be the right thing to do." She sighed deeply. "*Now* I'm going to go get dressed. Ma has been texting nonstop—the makeup lady is driving her crazy since I'm late."

Alina had neglected to mention that after landing in Srinagar, she and Emilio had gone to George's houseboat to invite him personally.

Alina had all but pleaded with him. "You have to come, George. It won't be complete without you, and it would mean so much to me."

George was quiet. The sunny, talkative man that she had known for the past few months was gone and there was a sadness in his eyes. He ran his hands through his hair, and to Alina, he looked old and forlorn. A man who had made peace with heartbreak. Much like her mother.

"I wish you both well. My love and blessings are with you,

Alina. I will try to make it. If you have time now, may I invite you both to eat with me? I would really love that." His smile returned for a moment when they agreed.

The meal was simple, the conversation anything but.

"Ma misses you, George," Alina said nonchalantly as they ate the rice and yogurt curry he had prepared. George kept his focus on his own plate and ate without saying a word.

Emilio added, "Alina's right, you know. She sold three paintings at auction, and each one of them had something to do with you. I don't understand art and even I could see that."

"You kids are thoughtful and kind. I love you for that. She's a remarkable woman. She's strong, and resilient. And look at how she raised you. I feel ... I just feel that I let her down." George's tone was gentle and filled with love.

"George," Emilio said. "You and Alina have a great friendship—from what she's told me and from what I've seen. To honor that friendship, we're asking you to be there. It would mean a lot to us, to Alina."

They left him with that. They told no one about the meeting.

The voice of Rami Sarkar snapped Alina back to the present. "Alina, why are you out here? You should be getting ready. I just sent Emilio to get ready too. You kids! This is your wedding day, why are you outside? We will take care of everything."

"Yes, yes, I am going to get dressed," she waved and smiled at him as she disappeared into her room.

Rami Sarkar had been a surprising godsend. After Alina and Sharmila apologized to him for not being more patient with him, they had asked to reengage his services for the finer details of planning the wedding. Rami agreed to organize the trips of friends and family coming into town and staying on the Sukoon, and he helped organize artists for Alina's henna.

In fact, the previous night, for Alina's mehndi henna night, Rami danced the most during the ritual. Sharmila, radiant in her rose saree, had sat holding Alina's hand steady to ensure that the henna lady could draw the intricate patterns. Suraj had sat by her side too, feeding her with his own hands as she sat with her arms outstretched for over three hours for the elaborate henna work.

Emilio's mother admired all the ornate decorations as they sat in the sun terrace of Qayaam Gah. "This is just marvelous. I have never seen anything like this in my life." The weather had cooperated, and several fire pits set around them were burning, dispelling the chill of early April.

Alina and Emilio's friends, Vikram's mother, Sharmila's sister, and Emilio's family all surrounded them and danced as the bride-to-be now waited patiently for the henna lady to finish the intricate patterns on her legs. Most of the henna dried quickly and Alina was grateful.

"I don't think I can sit still much longer," she said. "Ma, which patterns do you want?"

Sharmila refused. "Me? No way! This is for my dear child."

"Sharmila, come on, you should get some henna. In fact, let me pick it for you," Emilio said, and asked the henna artist to draw some peacock-shaped designs on Sharmila's hands.

When Suraj stepped away at the end of the henna ceremony, for the first time in months Sharmila asked Alina if she had heard from George. But before Alina could answer, her friends pulled her in to dance with them. Family and friends rejoiced in the pre-wedding revelry as live music and feelings of joy and hope filled the air.

Chapter 23

Alina and Emilio made their wedding entrance at the same time from opposite ends of the salon. The room roared with sounds of "we love you both" as friends and family rejoiced.

Sharmila walked in with Alina, and Emilio's mother accompanied him. The four walked in unison until they reached the center of the room.

Suraj handed the bride and the groom fragrant garlands of jasmine and roses. Alina took one garland and placed it around Emilio's neck, and he did the same for her. The cheers went up again.

Dressed in a shimmering red silk lehenga and adorned with Kashmiri silver earrings from Archana and a Rajasthani diamond choker from her mother, Alina looked picture perfect. Her curly hair was tamed into a bun with tiny crystals sprinkled over it.

Golden bangles adorned her arms. But her favorite piece of jewelry had been provided by Wajid. He had gifted her a sparkling silver payal set, anklets with tiny silver bells attached, that jingled gently as she walked.

"Please come to the mandap, my children." Sharmila beckoned them to sit at the official wedding mandap. Emilio's parents sat on one side of the bride and groom and Suraj and Sharmila sat together on the other side. Vikram's mother and Emilio's grandmother sat next to the mandap on comfortable chairs, as they had a hard time sitting on the floor. And Archana, their cousin from Betaab Valley, had made sure that the grandmas were comfortable, and most importantly, had the best view of the wedding ceremony.

"I love you," Alina whispered to Emilio as the priest began the wedding chants. The wedding ceremony was short but filled with custom and ritual. Emilio tied the symbolic mangalsutra around Alina's neck, a necklace that signified she was now a married woman. Alina had opted out of the vermillion powder that would have been placed in her hair, a typical sign of being married for Hindu women. The priest didn't object.

"I love you too, Alina."

The priest asked the couple to stand up. "This is the most ancient of our rituals. You already see the holy fire burning in this small hawan kund, a metal pot. You will walk around this fire seven times as I recite the prayers. With this walk, the shortest of your life, you will be tied together for the rest of this life and then the next seven ones. We have made a change that the bride and groom requested. Usually, the man leads the walk, and the bride walks behind him. But Alina and Emilio have chosen to walk each step together."

The couple rose and began to walk around the fire, holding hands as the priest recited prayers. Alina noticed her mother wiping away tears of joy. She squeezed Emilio's hand.

They finished the final round, and Emilio leaned over and kissed his bride on her forehead, then pulled her closer to whisper in her ear. "I adore you. And I've gotta say, you must have a special connection to your God."

Alina looked at him. "Special connection?"

"Yep. Look there." He subtly nodded towards the side of the mandap.

Standing in a far corner of the room, where Sharmila couldn't see him, was George, dressed in a black Nehru jacket, a rose in his right pocket. He caught Alina's eye, smiled, and mouthed, *Love you both.*

We love you too, she mouthed back.

Chapter 24

"Everyone, please have a seat. I would like to say a few words," Suraj said as the newlyweds made their way off the mandap and sat down just across from him. Sharmila was next to Alina, holding her hand.

"I didn't know he was going to make a speech," Sharmila said, adjusting her golden and peach saree. "Sitting on the floor in a saree is still hard, it messes everything up," she feebly joked.

"Yes, he told me he wanted to say a few words on behalf of dad. He's been working hard on this," Alina said, then leaned over to Emilio. She kept her voice low. "I think it's going to happen. Do you know if Wajid got—"

"Yes, amore, we're all set. Stop worrying, my wonderful wife. Everything is ready." Emilio squeezed her hand.

"It is not customary in this part of the world to make wedding toasts, and this is my first ever," Suraj said. "I hope I do okay. Alina, forgive any mistakes." He smiled brightly. "My brother Vikram would have loved being here today. I can only imagine how much love he would have showered on his daughter. I am not him, but I want to tell you, Alina, how much we all love you. Maulana Rumi used to speak of half-loves and as a young man,

I never quite understood that concept. I think he meant that human love always left a longing in us, and that it was the role of the Divine to make that half-love whole and complete. Today, as I see my lovely niece married to this amazing young man, I feel the presence of the Divine blessing their love to be whole, right here on earth, right now. On behalf of my brother Vikram and my entire family, we offer our blessings to the newlyweds. My prayer for you is that your love will reverberate not only across this lifetime, but across all your coming lifetimes."

There wasn't a dry eye in the room.

Alina blew kisses at Suraj, thanking him for his wonderful words. Then her relieved eyes found Wajid, who smiled and gave her a thumbs-up.

That was Alina's cue. She turned to her mother, whispering that she needed to go to the bathroom. "Can you come with me?"

The speeches stopped and during the couple of minutes while Alina was in the bathroom, Emilio joked about knowing he would always have to wait for her, even on their wedding day. Everyone laughed.

Suraj came back to the mic. "And now, everyone, if we could have your attention for a moment." He turned to Wajid, who was ready and waiting. The room became quiet, then suddenly all the lights went off, plunging the room into darkness.

Rami, who was handling the lights, directed a single spotlight toward Alina and Sharmila as they walked back into the salon.

Sharmila was confused. "Alina, what's going on?"

"Ma, this is exactly what should be happening," Alina said, praying this would work. Emilio, Suraj, and Wajid appeared by their side, holding a stunning canopy made of flowers. Alina kissed Sharmila on her forehead, then took a hold of the fourth corner of the canopy, the four of them lifting it high above Sharmila's head.

Sharmila now stood in the middle of the salon, surrounded by friends and family, with a canopy of fragrant flowers above her and the priest standing in front of her, microphone in hand.

"Alina, what's going on?" This type of canopy was for the bride before her wedding. It should have been for Alina.

Then she saw him.

George took the mic from the priest. "Hello, everyone. My name is George."

A chorus of *We know!*s answered him, and several people began clapping.

Sharmila turned to Alina. "What is happening?"

"Listen to him, Ma. For once, just listen to the man."

"Sharmila," George said. "My soul wasn't looking for another dancing partner, but then I met you. The past five months have been the hardest in my life as I tried to make peace with the fact I would never see you again. I tried to reason with myself—that I had loved and lost and that was to be my destiny. But, all I know is that I missed you. I am sorry. Will you ever forgive me?"

Sharmila felt her eyes well with tears.

George went on. "You made me want to live again, to laugh again, and you taught me to love again. And yes, kids, even at my age, love can still happen at first sight."

He put the mic down.

Sharmila watched George coming towards her. She had missed him—so much. Why hadn't she let herself admit that? Why had she forced herself to keep pretending? It was useless.

Right now, in this moment, it took everything she had not to run and hug him and kiss him as he approached. But she stood perfectly still as he continued.

"My dear Sharmila, I love you and trust our love. There is nothing in the world that I want more than to spend my life with you. Will you, my darling, do me the honor of a lifetime and marry me?" George was on one knee in front of her, holding up a single gold band.

Over the cheering of the entire wedding party, Sharmila could hear the familiar sound of her daughter crying. She could feel her own tears streaming down her face.

George beamed as he continued. "Do you remember the blessing we received about our knees staying flexible? I love you, my sweet Sharmila, but my knees … that blessing is still to come."

Sharmila laughed and held out her hand. George placed the ring on her finger, then stood up, pulled her close and kissed her forehead. He bent over and whispered in her ear, "I am so sorry."

She pulled back. She looked him in the eye and said, "I am sorry too."

He addressed the crowd again. "One thing I have learned is that the most precious thing we have is time. And I will honor the Indian tradition of chat magni pat vivaah today." Everyone clapped and cheered again at his reference to an old saying of *get engaged quickly and married quicker.*

As though on cue, the canopy was placed to the side and Wajid handed up wedding garlands for both Sharmila and George.

"Ma," Alina said, "only a fool would not be able to see the

love you have in your eyes for George. And I see the love that he has for you. It is my life's honor and privilege to give you away in marriage to a man I know loves you deeply."

Sharmila's and George's eyes met, and they held each other's gaze with love and tenderness. The garland exchange turned into another group hug. Then Wajid stepped in, asking George and Sharmila to sit down on the mandap and complete the wedding rituals.

The rituals completed, Alina and Emilio brought out the red pashmina shawl that Alina had ordered from the shop on the shikara on Dal Lake. The shawl, which had been embroidered with the names of everyone in Sharmila's and George's family—and Daneen and Vikram and so many more—was placed over the heads of the newlyweds. "Our combined love will always protect you," Vikram's mother blessed the couple.

"You knew about all this," Sharmila said to George as they shared a private moment under the shawl.

"I've known I wanted to marry you since the day I saw you fighting with Rami on Dal Lake. I just had to know that you had forgiven me. Then the kids told me about the paintings, and that you had painted me in them. That seemed like forgiveness. But," he added, slipping his hand into his jacket pocket, "I do have one confession to make."

Sharmila waited, smiling.

"There wasn't enough time to buy you a wedding gift. So for now, here you go." And he handed her her favorite chocolate bar.

Then he leaned in, and kissed his bride.

Glossary

Aba – Father

Antakshari – a party game in which each player must sing a song that begins with the last letter or syllable of the song sung by the previous player

Aru Valley – a spectacularly picturesque valley in Pahalgam, Kashmir; the Lidder River runs through it

beta – a term of endearment for a son

Betaab Valley – a spectacularly picturesque valley in Pahalgam, Kashmir; the Lidder River runs through it. Originally named Hagoon, it has been referred to as Betaab ever since a wildly popular Bollywood movie was filmed there

Chanderi-style silk – hand-loomed silk fabric with metallic threads woven into the fabric, for a brighter shimmer than plain silk

Char Chinari – literally, "the four sides"; an island in Dal Lake, location of a grove of ancient, supposedly magical Chinar trees

chat magni pat vivaah – "get engaged quickly and married quicker"

chicken biryani – a layered dish of chicken and basmati rice cooked together

chillai kalan – forty days of intense cold starting in December (i.e., winter)

chutney – a relish made with a variety of fruits, vegetables, nuts, and spices, sometimes cooked, sometimes raw, sometimes sweet and/or spicy

dal – the generic term for cooked legumes or pulses

Dal Lake – a beautiful lake in Srinagar, filled with floating gardens and surrounded by majestic mountains

dholak – a double-headed drum

dil – a term of endearment: heart; beloved

fanoos – a lantern-style hanging lighting fixture

fikar na karo – "don't worry"

gabba – a handmade rug, often with vibrant geometric or floral patterns

Gawkadal Bridge – a bridge in Srinagar, the site of separatist terrorist activities

Ghanta Ghar – the clock tower in the center of Lal Chowk, a local meeting spot

ghee – similar to clarified butter, but cooked until it develops a nutty flavor

gurudwara – A holy place of prayer that holds a copy of the Guru Granth Sahib, a Sikh holy book. The Gurudwara Chhevin Patshahi is one of the most important Sikh pilgrimage sites in Kashmir

haaq/haaq saag – a dish of greens (often spinach or collard greens) cooked with mustard oil, green chilies, and sometimes garlic

hakim – a wise naturopath healer

halwa – a fudge-like confection made from semolina flour, sugar, ghee, and water, flavored with a wide variety of nuts, spices, and sometimes chocolate

Hari Parbat – one of the world's tallest mountains, situated in the western Himalayas

hawan kund – a small metal open-top box in which a holy fire burns; used for weddings and other rituals

Hazratbal Mosque – an Islamic shrine, repository of a relic believed to be from the Prophet Muhammad

henna – a reddish-brown dye used for drawing intricate designs on skin

Jahun chhuh ashhun mazhar – "the world is a theatre of love"

jharoka – a stone window structure projecting out from an upper floor of a building's façade, overlooking the street; similar to a bay window

ji – a sign of respect added to the end of names

jodi – two people who do something together as a duo; a couple

kahwa – a traditional Kashmiri tea flavored with cinnamon, cloves, almonds, rose petals, and saffron

kajal kohl – a soft, deep black cosmetic used as eyeliner to create a sultry look

Kalij pheasants – a breed of bird native to Kashmir, almost as beautiful as peacocks

kangri – a personal charcoal-burning clay pot heater, worn under one's clothes

kebab – a skewer containing small pieces of meat, poultry, or fish, sometimes interleaved with vegetables, or vegetables alone, grilled over live fire

Khanqah-e-Molla – one of the oldest Islamic shrines in Kashmir, built on the banks of the Jhelum River in memory of a Sufi saint

Khauf-e-Asmaan– This is a fictional place. Terror in the sky

koi baat nahi – "no problem"

Lal Chowk – a vibrant shopping district in Srinagar

langar – a free meal provided to all, as an act of Sikh charity, often held after prayers

lehenga – a colorful, highly ornate type of wedding gown, often intricately beaded

lingam – a stone meant to symbolize the generative power of the god Shiva; sometimes thought of as a phallic symbol

mandap – a four-pillared structure under which the Hindu bride and groom sit; may be garlanded with flowers and decorated

mangalsutra – literally, "auspicious thread"; a thin necklace worn to signify that the bride is now a married woman

manji sahib – a platform in the middle of the worship room of a gurudwara (Sikh temple); it holds the copy of the Sikh holy book, and is raised above the worshippers to show respect

mehndi (henna) – the application of intricate designs to the hands, arms, and legs of the bride with nonpermanent dye; usually performed the night before the wedding, and accompanied by a party for all wedding-goers

Mughals – a Muslim dynasty that ruled most of northern India from the early 16th to the mid-18th century CE

nadur/nadur monje – a crisp fritter of lotus stems, fried and seasoned with fennel

Nigeen Lake – another scenic lake in Srinagar; sometimes considered part of Dal Lake, as they are connected by a strait

Nishat Bagh – literally "garden of joy"; one of many gardens on the eastern shore of Dal Lake

nonna – "grandma" in Italian

noonchai – a Kashmiri tea made with green tea and pink Himalayan salt

NRI – non-resident Indians; Indian citizens who live abroad

Nyay* – literally, "justice" – There is no organization by this name in Kashmir. This is fictional

pamposh – the Kashmiri water lily

pandit – literally, a wise and holy man

paneer – a dry fresh cheese made from pressed drained clabbered milk

parantha – an unleavened, many-layered flatbread, cooked on a griddle; sometimes a stuffing of spiced potatoes (aloo) is rolled in during layering.

pashmina – a very fine, lightweight, soft wool spun from delicate goat hairs; a shawl made from the material

payal – anklets hung with tiny silver bells, worn as an adornment

pheran – a tunic-like Kashmiri winter garment

phirni – a soft, sweet pudding made by cooking ground rice in milk with sugar, rosewater, or saffron, and sometimes nuts and/or sweet spices

posh puja – the end of the wedding ceremony, in which a red shawl or cloth is held over the heads for the bride and groom, and they are showered with flower petals; the ritual venerates the couple as if they were deities

Qayaam Gah – a luxurious retreat/resort in the Zabarwan Mountains overlooking Dal Lake and the Kashmir Valley

raad – floating gardens found on Dal Lake

rista – a traditional Kashmiri dish of the wazwan, lamb or mutton meatballs in a spiced red gravy

rogan josh – a curry with Persian origins, made with lamb or goat, tomato, yogurt, and a unique mix of spices

roop – the glowing skin a bride has

roti – a thin, round, unleavened flatbread, cooked on a griddle or in a skillet

saffron – the quintessential Kashmiri spice, which gives golden color and unique flavor to the food it is added to

salwar kameez – a matching outfit of a long (knee-length or longer) ladies' tunic (kameez) worn over pants (salwar); the kameez may be worn with separate, nonmatching pants or leggings

samosa – a savory pastry triangle filled with a potato, vegetable, or meat filling; may be fried or baked

sangeet – a prewedding tradition in which everyone sings and dances

sarangi – a stringed instrument

Shankaracharya Temple – a Hindu temple believed to have been built around 200 BCE; overlooking Srinagar, it is popular with locals and tourists alike

sherwani – A knee-length, fitted-waist tunic coat for men; may be ornately decorated for special occasions

shikara – a flat-bottomed wooden boat with a canopy over the seating and ornately carved hull, paddled from the rear by a boatman

SRK – shorthand reference to the Bollywood actor Shah Rukh Khan

sukoon – literally, "serenity"

tabak maaz – a dish of lamb ribs cooked until tender in broth with cardamom, fennel, ginger, and other spices, then fried in ghee until crisp on the outside; a traditional part of the wazwan feast

tchot – an oven-baked Kashmiri yeasted flatbread, similar to naan but with ridges across its top, a crisp crust, and chewy crumb

tiffin – a lunchbox, and the meal it contains

tilla – a style of embroidery unique to Kashmir, with intricate, raised designs, often using gold or silver threads

tosha – a sweet made of sugar, cashews, and almonds

trami – a communal plate, made of brass, on which shared food is arranged

wazwa – the chef responsible for preparing the wazwan; formerly only men were wazwas but now a few talented women are as well

wazwan – a traditional Kashmiri wedding feast of 20 to 40 dishes, many of them meat-based, cooked in large pots over a wooden fire

Zabarwan Mountains – a beautiful mountain range surrounding Dal Lake

zuva – literally, "soul mate"; the love of one's life

Acknowledgments

This book is my tribute to Kashmir and all the love stories it holds in its beautiful valleys. Kashmir to me has always been synonymous with love and I feel lucky to have been able to pen a story that reflects my deep attachment to this heaven on earth.

A huge thank you to Simi Jois for the beautiful photographs for marketing this book. A special thanks to our model.

A big, heartfelt thanks to my amazing muses who have kept me on the straight and narrow: Chef K.N. Vinod, Hadley Synylo, Anthony Hesselius, Monica Kharkar, Abhijeet Patil, Alyona Kapoor, Chef Sanjeev Kapoor, Chef Vikas Khanna, Ana Di, Niv Mani, Mollie Cox Bryan, Nivedita Sharma, Neha Garg, Shirin Gazdar, Aparna Phalnikar, Arti Bahl, Altaf Malik, Payal Sharma, Stephanie Sussan, Louise Romanchak, Stephanie Caruso, Marina Anderson, Mike Klozar (for the book's title) and Kathleen Flinn.

Thank you to Nandita Madan for painting the beautiful dancing bride that inspired the character of Sharmila.

To my dear Altaf Chapri, owner of Sukoon and Qayaam Gah – thank you for helping me with all the information about Kashmir, answering my million questions, and providing such valuable feedback.

Thanks also to Ramin Ganeshram for all her structural and editing help.

I want to thank my family and dear friends who encourage me and my crazy dreams.

To James aka Humble Nations for the cover art and design, Suzanne Fass, Graeme Hague, and Sandra Hume for editing this book. And Jason Anderson for book design.

My sons Jai and Arjun inspired me, and tirelessly encouraged me, to complete this book. My heartfelt thank you to both of them. They are my light and my reason for being.

About Monica Saigal (Bhide)

Equal parts storyteller and globe-trotter, Monica Saigal Bhide, an award-winning author, accomplished literary coach, and educator with over 15 years of experience, transcends countless borders—chronological, geographical, religious, and economical—to inspire her readers. Born in New Delhi, raised in the Middle East, and now residing outside Washington, DC, she currently serves as a corporate storyteller for one of the world's leading professional services companies. Her prolific portfolio, enriched by the many places she calls home, channels a distinctly cosmopolitan worldview.

Monica's words, which have appeared on renowned platforms including *The New York Times, The Washington Post, The Christian Science Monitor, Bon Appétit, Food & Wine,* and *Town & Country,* among others, are a collection of culture-driven articles that approach the world food first. Her books, all infused with a signature lyricism, consist of acclaimed cooking compendiums, like 2009's ***Modern Spice,*** brimming with contemporary versions of traditional Indian recipes. Her debut short story collection, ***The Devil in Us***, a clutch of spellbinding tales centered on fate and fortune, earned a spot on Amazon's bestseller list in 2015, while her more recent novel, ***Karma and the Art of Butter Chicken***, which explores the healing power of food, led NPR's café in Washington,

DC, to serve up creations inspired by her protagonist chef.

Her work has garnered numerous accolades and has been included in four Best Food Writing anthologies (2005, 2009, 2010, and 2014). Her memoir, *A Life of Spice*, was picked by Eat Your Books as one of the top five food memoirs of 2015. Top Chef's Padma Lakshmi picked Bhide's ***Modern Spice*** (Simon & Schuster, 2009), as one of the "Best Books Ever" for Newsweek in 2009. The Chicago Tribune named Monica "one of the seven food writers to watch in 2012."

In addition to her various storytelling endeavors, Monica appears as a regular voice on radio programs like NPR's "Kitchen Window," and recently launched "Powered by Hope," a podcast centered on life during a pandemic, and what it means to be physically distant yet connected to our very core. She also speaks about the intersection of food, culture, and writing for prestigious conferences and organizations such as the Smithsonian Institution, Sackler Gallery, Les Dames d'Escoffier, and Yale University. In 2013, she was appointed as Writing Coach in Residence for the Association of Food Journalists' annual conference, where she counseled writers on establishing their social media brands, underscoring her ultimate strengths as an eloquent, ever evolving, and outstanding writer.

Monica is a graduate of the George Washington University (Washington, DC), and holds a master's degree from Lynchburg College (Lynchburg, VA) and a bachelor's degree from Bangalore University (Bangalore, India). She feels fortunate for her rich, multicultural education and enjoys giving back to the global community by serving on committees and volunteering for Les Dames d'Escoffier, The International Association of Culinary Professionals.

Praise for Modern Spice (Simon & Schuster US, and Random House, India)

“Monica Bhide—a proven expert in all things South Asian—has compiled a witty and practical guide to Indian-style cooking. Her recipe for curried egg salad is alone worth the price of this book.”—*James Oseland, Editor-in-Chief,* **Saveur,** ***and author of*** **Cradle of Flavor: Home Cooking from the Spice Islands of Indonesia, Malaysia, and Singapore**

“For those of us who love Indian food and want to cook it at home, *Modern Spice* is the cookbook we've been waiting for. Monica Bhide's simple, flavor-packed recipes make this exciting cuisine modern, accessible, and right at home in the American kitchen.”— ***Victoria von Biel, Executive Editor,*** **Bon Appétit**

“The real spice in *Modern Spice* is love. No one writes about food with as much joy as Monica Bhide does. Her passion makes this book's beautiful stories and recipes a pleasure to read.”—***José Andrés, host of the PBS series “Made in Spain,” and author of the companion book*** **Made in Spain**

Praise for *The Devil in Us*

“Monica Bhide's excellent collection will transport you to unexpected places, moving you between America and India, hospitals, college campuses, ancient temples, a devastated train station. You will be entranced by the wide spectrum of characters she has created—a newlywed doctor learning to love his wife, a cancer survivor hoping for a second chance, a dying old man filled with hate, a transsexual who adopts a young orphan. Filled with surprises and heart, this book will pull you in and not let you go." —*Chitra Banerjee Divakaruni, author of* **Oleander Girl** *and* **The Mistress of Spices**

"Monica Bhide's beguiling writing takes us into the rich tapestry within private, intimate worlds that we don't want to leave." —*Shoba Narayan, James Beard Award finalist, author of the memoirs* **Monsoon Diary** *and* **Return to India**

"Monica Bhide's wonderful, internationally flavored collection is full of spice and life. The beguiling voice of a true storyteller will lure you out of yourself into her intriguing, fictional world. Enjoy." —*Diana Abu-Jaber, author of* **Crescent** *and* **Birds of Paradise**

Praise for *A Life of Spice*

"Monica writes stories about food, but often they are really stories about searching. She looks for what the world will reveal if you ask questions of the things we usually keep silent. She's a generous writer, seeking the finer, richer sides of us." —*Francis Lam, Editor-at-Large, Clarkson Potter, and New York Times Magazine columnist*

"Monica Bhide is more than a food writer. She's a chronicler of culture and family history. She is a romantic for the bond between parent and child. She is an essayist of her own heart and mind, fearlessly searching for the truth in both. She is endlessly fascinating to read." ***—Tim Carman, James Beard award-winning food writer for the* Washington Post.**

"Monica Bhide weaves magical spells with her words. Brilliantly describing cuisines & stories that echo the chimes of a faraway land while somehow simultaneously making one feel as if they are in her very backyard. Monica is magician with both words & food." ***—Chef Maneet Chauhan, judge on The Food Network's* "Chopped."**

Praise for *Karma and the Art of Butter Chicken*

"The past and present mingle in this charming story about the healing power of food." ***—Washington Independent Review of Books***

"... In *Karma and the Art of Butter Chicken* [Bhide] successfully turns her talents to the task of writing a consistently compelling and unfailingly entertaining novel, demonstrating her literary skills with deftly crafted and memorable characters embedded in a carefully constructed storyline of unexpected twists and surprising turns." ***—Midwest Book Review***

"Smell and taste your way through India while rooting for the protagonist to find a way to fill his hunger. When you put it down, find ways of reaching the hungry where you live."***—Edible Orlando***

"Monica Bhide has managed to blend her unique lyrical writing with an uplifting and powerful story of love and sacrifice. A beautiful book." **—Kathleen Flinn, author of the New York Times bestseller *The Sharper Your Knife, the Less You Cry***

Praise for *The Soul Catcher*

"*The Soul Catcher* is a mosaic novel packed with resilience and grief, magic and violence, love and loss. Bhide brings India to the page, wrapped in a beautiful sari but with tears in its eyes, a prayer in its mouth, and blood on its hands. This is a narrative about blessings that are curses and how pain changes us. A must read." **—Gabino Iglesias, author of *Coyote Songs***

"I couldn't stop reading this haunting, beautifully written book. Like a fairy tale, it begins with death and ends with life; Bhide's wise and empathetic voice guides us along the way, taking us on a journey through a series of interconnected lives, weaving them into an unforgettable story of love, redemption, and above all, kindness in all its forms—even the one we fear the most." **—Annia Ciezadlo, author of *Day of Honey: A Memoir of Food, Love, and War***

"Woven together with a tenuous strand of destiny, death, and beyond, *The Soul Catcher* is a collection of interconnected tales as dark as they are full of hope and redemption. Monica Bhide creates a compelling work that takes the reader through an epic journey through myth and magic that examines our relationship with fear, death, life, and love. A must-read." **— Kiran Manral, author**

Also by Monica Saigal (Bhide)

Inspirational Books

In Conversation with Exceptional Women (ebook)

Read, Write, Reflect (Bodes Well Publishing, 2018)

Fiction and Short Stories

The Soul Catcher (Bodes Well Publishing, 2021)

Karma and the Art of Butter Chicken (Bodes Well Publishing, 2016)

The Devil In Us (2014)

The Soul Catcher (Bodes Well Publishing, 2017)

Tattletales (Bodes Well Publishing 2017)

Food Essays and Cookbooks

A Life of Spice (2015)

Modern Spice: Inspired Indian Flavors for the Contemporary Kitchen (Simon and Schuster, 2009; Random House India, 2010)

The Everything Indian Cookbook: 300 Tantalizing Recipes from Sizzling Tandoor Chicken to Fiery Lamb Vindaloo (Adams Media, 2004)

Monica's essays have been included in *Best Food Writing 2005, 2009, 2010,* and *2014*, edited by Holly Hughes (Da Capo Press)

Monica's books are available through Amazon.com, BN.com, Kobo, iBooks, and her website, monicasaigal.com

Made in the USA
Middletown, DE
20 February 2024